THE MORASS
SERVANT OF THE FLY GOD

ZACHARY ASHFORD

Let the world know:
#IGotMyCLPBook!

Crystal Lake Publishing
www.CrystalLakePub.com

WELCOME
TO ANOTHER

CRYSTAL LAKE PUBLISHING
CREATION

Join today at www.crystallakepub.com & www.patreon.com/CLP

PROLOGUE

PROVIDENCE, SERENDIPITY, or good fucken luck, whatever you called it, Calvin Pastroni saw the broken-down campervan as nothing but an opportunity. The driver was isolated, caught miles from civilization with no shelter and no protection. The chances of another vehicle passing by were slim and only eagles patrolled these plains with any regularity, observing the rising hills in the distance and the dry creek-beds and dusty pastures below with the hungry eyes of predators ready to swoop in, snatch away, and kill. The sole building between the van and population was an abandoned farmstead given to rot and ruin. And that was exactly what had encouraged Pastroni to choose this place when he'd come looking for prey this far from home. Recent paper talk meant people were finally paying attention to the disappearances occurring in his usual hunting grounds. However, the rains were still coming, and that meant he had to persevere if he wanted to fulfil his promise, so it was good that stranded out here, the sheila pulling bags from the van could be taken without a single soul knowing.

The fly alighting on his windscreen buzzed its wings and cleaned its proboscis, and he smiled. He'd brought this one from Mother's room. There was every chance she had blessed it, that it too knew what was coming. Pastroni scratched absently at an infected pimple on his chin, checked his rotten teeth in the rear-view mirror, and held a finger out to the insect. It took to the air. Landed on his thumb. Kissed him.

The girl pointedly did not look at him, and he knew that he had to get out of the vehicle before making things too weird for her. He didn't want her to think that he was some Ivan Milat type. That always made life harder, and he couldn't afford to have his purpose scuppered by a glorified rapist and gun nut. No, he had to remain vigilant and careful, or else everything his mother had worked towards would be wasted.

He waved politely at the girl and slid his gun, a Colt .357, underneath his seat. He finally got out of the Ranger and approached. "G'day," he said. "Come a cropper?"

The girl, a short dumpy sheila in her early twenties, looked at him, her eyes wild. Her shoulders heaved. She took a deep breath, and spewed words at rapid speed. "It came out of nowhere! I tried to swerve, but it went the other direction, and . . . my boyfriend went looking for help and now my phone is dead."

Boyfriend? Time to think intelligently. No witnesses. No *mistakes*. "Hey, hey, chill out," Pastroni said. "How long ago'd old mate leave? I'll go get him."

She looked north along the empty highway. "A while. Not long." She was all over the shop. Had an accent too, not that he could pick it. All those Euro accents sounded the same. German or French or something in between. Nevertheless, something had shaken her up pretty good. "First, let's have a gander at the vehicle and make sure it's not gonna burst into flames." It wouldn't, but she didn't need to know that. "If it's not something I can fix, I'll tow you into town. We'll get your fella on the way, whaddaya reckon?"

She wiped a tear from her eye. "I would be very grateful!"

He nodded, mindful of keeping his distance. A little more bullshitting, and he could get her in the Ranger and alleviate any risk of someone driving by and seeing anything. "Just the two of you?"

"Yes. We thought that if he went to look for help and I waited here, someone might come along."

He put on his most compassionate expression. "Crikey love, that's a bit bloody risky."

"What do you mean?"

"You fresh off the boat, are you? Even the flies out here bite. And they're the least of your worries. Dingoes the size of cattle. Fucken pythons that'll swallow you whole. *Drop bears*."

She raised an eyebrow. "I know about drop bears! They're *not* real."

"Tell my Uncle Barry that."

She looked at him, concerned; curious. "You are joking. You don't have an Uncle Barry."

"Not any fucken more I don't! Bloody drop bear got him!" His laughter boomed in the vast Outback silence.

The girl smiled awkwardly.

"Let's see the damage then. What's your name?"

"Simone, but my friends call me Simi."

Her friends? Crikey. Talk about trusting. The front of the van was a wreck. They'd hit a huge buck kangaroo and they'd hit it hard. Sprawled across the bonnet and lodged halfway through the windscreen, it had met an uncomfortable demise. It's one unbroken leg twitched. Blood ran down what was left of the headlight and hissing radiator. The creature's guts had opened as it plunged through the glass. Intestines and the remnants of half-digested leaves and grass steamed on the hot metal of the hood. Its head and muscular torso hung loosely over the passenger seat. Blood oozed out of the shredded lacerations and pooled in the footwell.

He grabbed it by the tail and heaved. The glass didn't release its grip. He picked up a rock and pummeled the glass around the marsupial with an explosion of sudden violence, widening the gap. He heaved again. The roo flopped to the ground. "Jumped as you collected it, did it?"

She nodded. "I thought I was going to die."

"Not yet."

Her eyes dilated. "Excuse me?"

"If we don't get you out of here, you bloody might. Your car's been shit-mixed and you don't wanna stay overnight. Could be days before someone comes along. Thirst, hunger, dehydration. Horrible way to go."

"Can we tow the car? It's a rental."

He dropped to his knees before the van and looked underneath the vehicle. "You're gonna be spewing, but nah. Them axles are cactus. Steering's shot. No clue about your brakes. Once we get to town, you'll have to call someone."

"Do you have a phone?"

"Me? Nah. Track you, listen to you. Fuck that."

He climbed to his feet and went to the Ranger. He paused before opening the driver door.

Simi hadn't moved.

"You coming? Don't get me wrong, take your chances, but I've gotta be honest . . . you'd be bloody silly to stay."

She hesitated.

Pastroni drummed his fingers on the chassis. "Come on . . . hop in and help me find your man. What's his name again?"

"Gabor."

He laughed rudely. "Don't you have proper names in Germany?"

She pursed her lips. "I'm Swiss. He's Hungarian."

"Well, it's just gone lunchtime!" When he saw she wasn't laughing, he shook his head and plopped into the driver's seat. "In you get." He opened the passenger door. "Fucken Gabor. Fair dinkum."

Simi looked at the filthy vehicle with disdain. She wiped the seat, tried to shoo the fly out the door, and sat. The fly moved to the driver's visor. "He went that way." Simi said, pointing.

"No wukkas." Pastroni steered onto the road. "Sorry about the lack of music. Radio brainwashes you. Fucken bad news this, chaos that. It's too much. About time God sorted it out."

Simi sat up rigidly and fingered the door handle.

He waited for a response. When it didn't come, he toyed with his rear-view mirror, checking there was no one behind. Through the steel grate he'd installed behind the front cab, he could see the coast was clear. When he returned his gaze to the road, a solitary figure had appeared beyond the heat-haze mirages, shimmering on the blacktop.

"That's him!" Simi said.

Pastroni tooted his horn and caught up to Gabor. As soon as he'd parked the car, Simi thrust open the passenger-side door and ran to her boyfriend. Pastroni let them have their moment.

Simi talked frantically, gesturing at him.

Gabor, who was small enough to be a jockey, waved awkwardly.

The fly buzzed erratically. Pastroni stepped out of the Ranger, hitched his shorts and scratched his balls. "You want that ride?"

"Is it much farther?" Simi asked.

"Too bloody far to walk, I'll tell you that for free."

Gabor shot him a challenging glance. "We'll take our chances. It'll be an adventure."

Pastroni spat a loogie so thick it was almost a complex organism. He squeezed a sore on the back of his neck and shook his head. "Honestly, mate, I can't allow it. Be dark in an hour or two. Gets real fucken cold out here."

Simi tugged at Gabor's arm. Said something.

"We really appreciate it," Gabor said. "But we're fine. Honestly."

"Are you sure, it's pretty bloody sketchy out here. You don't know who's gonna come along these roads. Haven't you seen movies?"

Gabor whispered something to Simi and turned back to Pastroni. "It'll be a story to tell. What's the point of coming to the Outback without getting off the beaten path a little."

"You're gonna be following tarmac, Gabes. Dunno if they have that in Hungaria or not, but it's the very definition of beaten path. Fair go, but, if you wanna see the parts of the bush folks usually don't, I can show you some amazing shit."

"Just take no for an answer," Simi said, her voice shaking with fear.

"Fuck me silly, you two think I'm some big bloody weirdo backpacker murder bloke." He raised his hands in placatory fashion. "Let me start again."

Simi tugged Gabor's arm again. This time, Gabor took her hand and nodded. "It's fine," he told her. He turned to Pastroni, "We really don't mean any offense, but we're just going to walk until we find a phone and call the rental company. We paid for insurance on the vehicle. You understand, of course."

"You're taking a silly risk. There are fucken dingoes out here and everything. They're not real friendly. Ate a baby once, you know."

"Please, Sir," the Hungarian said. "We really don't want to impose."

"You're not imposing. I *insist*."

Gabor looked awkwardly at his feet. Shuffled. Looked at Simi, who was edging away.

"That's not all, is it? You've got something you want to say," Pastroni said.

Gabor looked away. "Well, I don't want to be impolite, so it is better to say nothing."

"Nah, nah, fucken nah. Say it. There's no hurt feelings here."

Gabor stared into Pastroni's eyes. "We would rather take a risk with the dingoes than get in your car." He held his gaze.

Pastroni's chest hitched. His head buzzed. Who did this little peckerhead think he was? "Have it your way, you silly prick."

Both backpackers looked shocked. Gabor raised his palms in a conciliatory gesture. "We don't want any trouble."

Simi said something to the Hungarian.

"You have our bags in your car," Gabor said.

"Get 'em out then."

Gabor edged closer. "We didn't mean to offend you."

Simi kept her distance.

Pastroni grinned.

"Unlock it please," Gabor's voice shook as he tried the handle.

Pastroni's smile widened. "Whaddaya scared of mate?"

"Please just unlock the back door."

"Rightio." Pastroni reached down as if to pop the latch. The fly landed on it; he snatched up his gun instead. He stepped wide of the Ranger, leveling the weapon.

Simi screamed. "Gabi!"

Gabor spun his head towards her; towards Pastroni. Towards the Colt.

"Boo!" Pastroni said.

Gabor raised his hands. "Please. We—"

The gunshot didn't echo. It boomed and the soundwaves disappeared into the vast Outback emptiness. The back of Gabor's head blew out, exploding in a mess of chunked bone and brains that slopped to the dusty ground with plopping noises. His leg twitched like the kangaroo's had. The fly landed on the hole in his face. Feasted.

Pastroni laughed.

Simi, screaming like a curlew, burst into a sprint.

Pastroni giggled. She was far from athletic. He hefted Gabor's prone body into the Ranger. "Fucken Gabor. Your mum should have had the respect to give you a real name like bloody Wazza or Shane. Deadset."

He closed the boot and kicked dirt over the gore littering the ground. He stepped casually into the driver's seat, accelerated, and spun the car to a skidding stop in front of the fleeing girl.

She screamed, turned, ran the other direction.

He stomped the pedal, circled her, and slammed on the brakes. "Love," he said, leaning out of the driver's window, keeping the gun pointed directly at her. "Simi. See reason. I need you, and this . . . well, this can go easy for you, or this can go hard . . . "

"I won't tell anyone."

"They all say that—"

"You can believe me! You can believe me!" Her words were hyperventilated gasps.

"Yeah, but love, I mightta been able to believe them too. I wouldn't know though because it's not fucking happening. Get in the back."

She ran for the road. *For crying out loud.* He accelerated, catching up to her in a matter of seconds, and this time, he nudged her with the nose of the Ranger. She sprawled to the ground. When she came to a stop, she clutched her hip and howled at the sky. In fairness, it would have hurt.

He parked the car beside her and got out. He hefted her up by her hair and twisted her head to face him. "I've warned you, Simi. I need you to get in the back and keep Gabor company. You're an important part of my plans, and I'm taking you home to Mum, so keep quiet and I won't hurt you any more than I have to."

Hours later, back at his property, Pastroni parked outside an old Titan shed and spun to face Simi. Trapped in the back with her dead boyfriend, she had reached a state of shock. The fly rested on her hair, cleaning Gabor's blood from its forelegs.

"Honey, we're home!"

Simi stared at Gabor's ruined skull.

"Don't be like that," Pastroni said. "It's time for church." He popped open the back door and casually leaned inside to grab the girl.

"Stay away from me!"

She slapped his hand, and in turn, he cuffed her across the face. When she collapsed on Gabor, he grabbed her left leg and tugged hard. She tumbled out of the vehicle with a thud, screaming in pain.

"In a way, you're a bit like that kangaroo, you know. You were just there minding your business on that bit of highway when the wrong bloody vehicle came along. A little bit later, and here you are. Still, at least you'll die for a purpose."

She sobbed. He had no fear she would try to run.

He guided her to the shed where she would be assailed with the true face of beauty. From within, a thick buzzing sound rose and fell. The shed, the air itself, seemed to vibrate with the sound. "It's good you've stopped fighting, because this is a happy moment," he said. "Now have a look at this."

He slid open the door and the volume swelled into a cacophony. Flies skittered around in the space before the curtain. Their bodies thwacked into it with plopping thuds. The curtain billowed in the breeze and thousands of flies zoomed around the room as he pulled back the curtain. Slowly, as the chaos of darting black shapes settled, the propped-up corpse of his mother loomed. Her empty eyes stared. Her leathery skin glistened in the halogen light. Flies buzzed around her in a perverted aura. "G'day, Mumsy. The drive was worth it. We've got one, and this time, I think it's gonna work. It's gonna be a wet summer, and I've got a real good feeling about this."

Simi shied away, sobbing. "Is that what you're going to do to me?"

He looked at her like she was crazy. "Are you *serious*?" He gestured at his dead mother. "She was a *princess*. The finest lady to walk the Earth. The one who taught me about God and how we could help in his rebirth. There's no way you get the same treatment she does. Have some bloody respect!"

He guided her to an empty weight bench and forced her to sit before handcuffing her to it and plucking a Bowie knife and a bottle of murky liquid from a shelf. "You," he said. "You get to be a part of the ceremony. Open wide and drink this."

The handcuff chain jerked and rattled as Simi tried to stand. She crashed back down. Pastroni had learned from past mistakes and invested in industrial-standard to make sure no one could escape once they were in his captivity. Simi tried to twist away. She thrashed. She screamed. She threw her body back and forth. The bench wobbled. He'd bolted it to the floor, but repeated straining over time would test any fixture, let alone one installed by someone as careless as he was.

She kicked out, but Pastroni was wise to that as well. He stood back and when her feet dropped, he swooped in and grasped her hair. He pressed the knife across her throat. "It's just a bit of holy water. Settle down, love."

She clenched her teeth. Pressed her lips together.

He squeezed her chin, pried open her mouth with the tip of the knife, levering it between teeth. When she relented, he upended the bottle. Water washed into her gob. He clamped her jaw shut. Forced her to swallow.

Simi shook violently.

"Hey! Hey! Hold still. You'll make it worse on yourself if you resist."

The girl continued to shake. The bench wobbled to and fro. He'd need to see to that shonky bolt before it caused him more grief. He yanked her head back and drew the blade across her throat. At first, the blood welled in a polite ribbon, but as she tried to scream, it came out in gurgling bubbles, running down her collarbone and onto the floor. The flies homed in on it.

When he thought she was just about dead, he wiped his hand in the blood and then caressed his mum's lips with his slick fingers. "This time, I'll get my baptism, Mum. I can feel it." He kissed his silent mother on the forehead and turned back to Simi. "I'll see you in a few hours, Mum. It's gonna happen this time. I promise."

He uncuffed Simi and dragged her to a blanket. He promptly rolled her up in it and threw her over his shoulder.

When he finally made it to the holy ground, thick waves of undulating flies billowed above the morass like the black robes of cultists at an arcane ceremony. They rippled and pulsed in their thousands, congregating. He had never seen them in such a mass. They were louder and more inquisitive than ever before, and he knew that the time for ascension was upon him. They buzzed and flicked, landing on his blood-spattered shirt to clean their proboscises and to revel in his stench.

His heart swelled with anticipation as he enjoyed the sensation of them fluttering on his skin and he smiled as he dropped Simi only a few feet from the murky water's edge, a gift for the invisible creature his mother had told him about. Flies skittered away from the corpse, buzzing and droning beneath the burning sun, reticent to loiter near the offering.

He inhaled deeply, savoring the cloying aromas and waited for some sign that God was aware of his presence. He picked his nose with a calloused thumb, inspected the booger he had dislodged, wiped it on the inside of his pocket, and exhaled, blowing wheezing air through the cleared nostril.

He was aware of the abandoned brick building, squat and still on the other side of the swamp, but he paid it no more mind than he had on any of his other weekly pilgrimages. Officially, it was an abandoned radio repeater, but those were kept on high ground, and the beeping blips he sometimes heard from within would have fallen silent if it was true. It didn't matter, though, it wasn't watching *him*. If it was, he'd have been intercepted long ago. The Swiss girl wasn't the first he'd fed to the swamp, to the heavenly body he believed it hid. Instead, he took the building's existence as proof his mother was right. This *was* a meteor field and the beast waiting beneath the surface was biding its time until it had a servant it could trust, and the earthly conditions were right. The authorities didn't know this, though. No, the God was his secret, and once, before she'd transcended, it used to be his mother's.

He tapped the mire with the sole of his leather boot and stepped back from the lapping, squelching movement of the sludge. When it settled, he untied the blanket and rolled Simi out of its embrace. He yanked her towards him by her hair and a hunk of her love-handle. He groaned as he hefted her up. He rolled her onto his knee, shuffled closer to the patient murk and heaved, throwing her as far into the swamp as he could. Concentric circles swelled outwards in a slow-moving wave. Flies, disturbed by the motion, rose from the swamp like incense from a thurible and landed on the corpulent body, pushing it down with their combined weight. Slowly, she sank beneath the glugging surface, pockets of air bursting and farting in time with her slow immersion.

Pastroni stood to attention. He wiped his hands on his blue shorts and scratched his balls. Another job well done. Mum would love what he'd done here. She'd have loved how he did the whole thing in front of her too. All of it. He wiped sweat from his brow, and when he turned to the house where Mother would be waiting for him, something splashed.

When he thought no further movement would come, the swamp bubbled and gurgled. A foul stench emanated upwards, and then, underneath, where the clarity was minimal, something thrashed. The flies tornadoed, droning in the humid air. Momentarily, he thought he saw a fin break the surface, but as quickly as it had exploded into action, the dirty marsh stilled again.

A single fly, however, did not. It hovered in front of him before landing on his wiry moustache. It gamboled on his lip and crawled to his nostril. He snorted. Spun backwards, certain he'd heard someone whisper behind him. Only a cloud of flies hovered there, black and ominous. Hot breath misted on the base of his neck. He spun again, his heart staccato.

See.

"Who's there?" He spun, looking for the source of the voice; certain someone had found his dumping ground.

Here, in the water.

The black morass lapped on the shoreline. Again, he thought he saw the curve of something primal beneath the surface. Hoped the girl he'd dumped there wouldn't float to the top. He'd put enough holes in her to make sure she sank, but you never knew. Corpses were funny things.

The buzz of flies swelled again. They whirled around him before landing on his face, his ears, his bare hands and his shins. The swamp was thankful and would bless him for this sacrifice. When the insects disappeared, he stepped forward. A swirling black orb coalesced above the murk. Made entirely of flies, it hovered, an eye staring deep into his devoted soul. It swelled and contracted. Darkened. Black insects peeled off the shape and swarmed around his head in a halo. Something his mother had long ago prophesied was happening: a sign from God.

Pastroni dropped to his knees and the flies swarmed again. He dropped his head into the water; a self-baptism in the swamp where he'd dumped so many lost souls.

The water churned and thrashed, and a white shape, long and segmented, appeared. It reared from the water. He wiped dripping liquid from his hair and looked up in awe. It was true. Everything his mother had taught him was true and he thought of her flyblown corpse, propped like a statue and wired into place in his shed. She was right and he was blessed. What a beautiful world!

He laughed, and the swirling fog of flies replicated the sound in pitch perfect accuracy. The roiling tumor stretched towards him, and as he gawped at their movement, they gagged him, piling into his mouth, down his esophagus, into his lungs and out of his nostrils. They filled him and feasted on him, and the giant thing in the morass spoke to him as it made promises he could not refuse.

When it was all over, he kneeled on the shore, palms out in supplication, thrilled at the providence he'd been afforded. He knew what it wanted and what he had to do. Through him, God would be reborn.

ONE

KIP CRINKLED THE half-empty cigarette, dropped it into his pack of Winnie Blues, stirred the tobacco through the already half-chopped narb and poured the contents of the bowl into the grinder. Finger hovering over the button, he toed Gus in the thigh. "Crank it," he said, nodding to the stereo.

Gus rolled his eyes, leaned over to twist the volume dial and continued noodling the guitar. He nodded his head in time with the main riff of Refused's "Summerholidays Vs. Punkroutine" and fingered his way through a piss-poor approximation of it. "Used to know how to play this one." He rearranged his grip on the fretboard. "We should play another gig before you go, dude."

Kip scraped the dust from the side of the grinder and dropped it into the bowl of weed. He pictured the scene. A garage party on one of the properties out here somewhere. Cars on blocks in the front yard. Horses in the paddock. A bunch of rednecks and tarts who'd rather listen to some inbred poke sing about his dog leaving him. "Nah, man, leaving in the morning. I'm supposed to move in to the flat down there by Wednesday to make first practice. These dudes are pros, I can't fuck them about . . . besides, the chicks around here don't get it. They all think it's too hardcore, man. Think we're, like, criminals or some shit." He packed the first cone. "Can't fucken wait to hit Brissie. Scene down there, I'm gonna be knee-deep in clunge by the time I've played a few shows." He sparked the lighter and held it to the billy; got a nice red cherry burning. The bong bubbled and then popped as he inhaled the thick swirl of smoke.

"Can't believe you've scored a gig with Primordial Effigy. They're like royalty, dude."

Kip thumb-screwed the fattest cone he could and passed it to Gus. The guitarist was right. It was crazy they'd chosen him to be their new guitar-player. He was easily the biggest no-talent loser out of everyone in his own shitty little regional band, The Pork Snorkels. "I can't help if I killed it when they needed stand-in guitars in Rocky, my man."

Gus shook his head. "Modest as always. Just remember me when you're nailing groupies on the tour-bus. Wait, that sounded wrong. Remember me *after* you've nailed them."

"Thinking of you at any time is an instant soft-on."

"Yeah, well, your mum doesn't think so."

Laughter. "C'mon, man, is it a bong or a microphone?" Kip flicked the MacGyvered Orchy bottle to hurry his friend along. Gus loved to bloody chat while he held onto the billy; it was his fatal flaw. While he sucked on the densely packed cone, Kip ran through the first meeting with the dudes from Primordial Effigy for the ten-thousandth time. It was some proper Henry Rollins shit. He'd been handing out free cassette tapes of Pork Snorkels' debut EP when Levels and Tim burst into the bar in a panic. Levels had seen the black-clad rockers sitting near the smoke machine and come straight over. "Yo, does anyone know our songs? Rennie's been arrested." He hadn't taken two seconds to consider he'd be playing support with the Snorkels beforehand; he'd immediately volunteered. Now, here he was hanging out with Gus for what would be the last time in ages.

His mate hacked his way through the cone, coughing and spluttering. "Pack it deep enough, you bastard?" His eyes were like piss-holes in the snow and his dopey grin stretched from ear to ear.

Kip laughed and packed himself a more moderately sized cone. "I'm gonna fucken miss you, cunt."

"It'll be 'right, mate. You think I wanna float around this shithole forever? Keep working in the bloody abattoir? Soon as I get the chance, I'll come down to Bris-Vegas."

"Don't call it that. Only wankers call it that, mate, seriously." He choofed and served another for Gus. "I suppose you'll have to come down for the first gig. Be, like, the guest of honor or some shit."

"Yeah, man, I spose I will. I spose I will." Gus smoked the billy and checked his watch. "You'd better show me this bike, mate. Gonna need to get back to the misso before long."

Kip led Gus outside to his little Kawasaki EL250. The stickers on the plastic fairing were bleached by years of exposure to the sun and foam poked through cracks in the leather. "She looks a bit rough, but she's in good nick engine-wise."

"Fucken hope so. Longreach to Brisbane's a long haul on a 250. You'd be better off getting the bloody train."

As far as Katy was concerned, this backpacking thing was a blast, but holy shit, it was good to get her feet off the hot tarmac. If she was in the sun much longer, the soles of her shoes were gonna melt. She buckled her seatbelt and smiled happily at the driver. Heat or no heat, she was ticking off all the places in her grandfather's journal in no time. "Thanks so much," she said. "You're a brave lady picking up a backpacker out here in the country."

The old woman's thin purple hair, curled like a shower loofa, shook as the car travelled onto the highway and over a pothole. "Yeah, I'm brave, but you're a bloody idiot, lovey. What's a pretty little thing like you hitchhiking on these roads for?" She lowered the driver's window and stuck her arm out like a truckie. "The bloody psychos on this road'll take a little sheila like you and no one'll hear from you till you're found in a pile of croc poo."

"You think there are serial killers out here in the sticks?" She pulled a notepad out of her jacket pocket.

The old duck screwed her face into a crumpled mess of wrinkles and sunspots. "What's with the pad?"

Katy was no stranger to the cynicism of the country locals, which didn't go as far as a mistrust of intellectualism, but was certainly suspicious of it. She went to the spiel. "It's why I'm out here. I'm writing a book on the 'characters' of the Aussie Outback. Despite what movies and the papers tell us, there's a lot more to the people who live out here than bloody murder and cattle-farming, I reckon."

"And you want me to be in this book?"

"Maybe." So far, she'd found while most people out here were friendly, they were reticent to talk on the record. "My Pop left me a book, you see. He'd travelled the Outback as a fruit-picker. He recorded everything in his journal and, well, he knew I was studying journalism and before he kicked the bucket, he gave it to me. I'm trying to hit every one of the locales he went to."

"So, you don't want me in it?"

She realized she hadn't asked the driver's name. "Sorry, I've been rude. I'm Katy."

The pink-haired driver pulled her free hand from the window and turned her eyes from the shimmering haze of heat coming off the road ahead to look her in the eye. Then she shook Katy's hand. "Maude. Do you want me in this bloody book or not? I've lost me train of thought."

"Well, Maude, I'd say there's a good chance. I haven't been at it long and I haven't met too many sheilas on the road yet. It's mostly been truck-drivers named Darren or Bruce . . . "

"Good name, Bruce. My boy's named Bruce."

"Of course, anyway, I can't definitively say yeah, but there's potential. If you're happy to."

Maude picked her teeth. "Go on then. What was I talking about before you went off on your tangent?"

"Croc poo."

Maude grinned. "Exactly my point. You're here wandering the roads and taking notes on the people of the Outback, but there's at least three kids gone missing this year: two girls and a fella. Not a sign of any of 'em."

Katy smiled. "Let me guess: they were all young? This is what I'm talking about. As soon as anyone north of the Sunny Coast goes missing people are searching for another murderer. You don't think it's possible these kids only want to escape the endless vista of dust and highway?" Seriously, though, it was crazy these old ducks didn't realize how much better life was in the city. It was like they'd been out here their whole lives and had no clue what was on offer for them where the roads were made of tarmac and the buildings weren't three kilometers away from each other.

"Look, missy, I know you don't know what you're talking about, so I'm gonna give you some free advice. If you want us 'country-folk' to warm to you, you're best not to patronize us."

She'd done it again. Dad always told her she was a smug little shit; reckoned it was something else she'd got from her granddad. "Sorry, I didn't mean . . . "

"Don't apologize. As I said, I don't care, and I understand what you're thinking. Lots of kids do leave the towns and head to Brisbane or the real cities further down south, but when they do, they let us know. These girls are missing. Do you know what they were doing when they disappeared?" Maude held a finger up to shush Katy. "They were hitchhiking."

Man, it was like one of her grandma's lectures. "Yeah, but—"

"You want my advice, young lady; you find a better way to travel. Now, I want you to write this bit down. You quit this hitching shit before one of your rides doesn't stop where you want it to."

Katy tapped her pen on the pad's spiral binding. "So, yes, you do believe there are serial killers out here?"

Maude pushed the auxiliary lighter in, heating it up, and plucked a smoke from the open box in her pocket. "You'd better believe it, Missy. Next question."

TWO

LEI NGUYEN HATED this part of the job. Sitting awkwardly at an outdoor setting on the Cambridge family verandah, she wished she could be anywhere else in the world. Unfortunately, she'd drawn the short straw and she had to be the one to hand over the information. "We're reasonably sure this matches one of the shoes in the photo you gave to us." Inside the plastic bag on the timber table, a single pink Converse sneaker, weather-beaten and muddy, rested on its worn sole. "I hate to ask this, and I want you to know I've been in your shoes, so please, take your time responding, but does this look familiar."

"Yeah, it's hers. Where was it?"

For Nguyen, this was a sight she'd never be able to take as stoically as Colin, Dana's father, was trying to. She got it. Living out here, growing up on this farm and going to school with the other cattle-wrangling, camping, farming boys of the Outback, emotions were weakness to a man like him, but he should be feeling it. He should be taking it in and expressing his thoughts like his wife, like Dana's mother Debbie was.

Debbie was practically melting, had clearly already resigned herself to the fact she wasn't going to see Dana again. It wasn't necessarily true, but Nguyen, who hoped desperately her own brother would one day be found, had to admit it was beginning to look like Debbie's suspicions might be right.

Nguyen nodded, reached a hand across the table to grasp Debbie's.

Chase Coghlan, Nguyen's partner, opened the manila folder on the desk in front of him and pulled out a photocopied page of the Queensland highways map. He'd circled a spot on the Landsborough Highway out near the Macsland Rest Area.

Colin inspected it. "What the fuck was she doing all the way out there?"

Debbie broke into fresh sobs.

Nguyen waited for Colin to comfort her. "We're not sure, yet, and we want to stress this: at the moment we have no further information." She hated lying with a passion, but they were on strict orders here. Ever since pricks like Ivan Milat and Bradley Murdoch had become such intense news stories, cops like her had to play their cards close to their chest. The only saving grace she could console herself with was the extra upset wouldn't do the Cambridges any good.

Coghlan interrupted. "We want you to know we're doing everything we can, and you'll be the first to know if we can offer any solace, or even . . . even any resolution to your unrest."

Debbie's shoulders heaved again.

Nguyen looked at her partner as if he was the dumbest bastard in the country.

Colin shook his head. "Well, thanks a fucken lot, mate. What have you found apart from a shoe? Our girl's gone missing. People are saying she's fallen victim to the same prick the other two girls did and you offer resolution and a single fucken sneaker. You're too busy getting people for speeding on the highway instead of doing your real job; is that it?"

Coghlan gathered the documents.

"We're acutely aware this is a trying time, Mr Cambridge, but please, Chase meant no harm. He's just shit with his words." Her partner at least had the good grace to look embarrassed, which helped as she continued. "At the moment, we have no reason to believe your daughter—"

"Dana. Her name is Dana."

"—no reason to believe Dana has been abducted. There is firm evidence of the other two abductions. Well-documented evidence. There are plenty of reasons for a runaway to get rid of their shoes, particularly if they're easily identifiable." What Nguyen didn't say was the documentation regarding the other girls had come from the newspapers and they'd only been silenced through a court injunction. Although the evidence they had about Dana wasn't firm, it was suggestive.

"She's not a runaway," Debbie said.

Nguyen straightened her collar.

"She left too much here to be a runaway; even the packet of smokes and box of frangers she thinks I don't know about. She was a little shit, but she wasn't a runaway. Something's happened to her, and the sooner you lot are straight with us, the easier this'll be."

Nguyen's cheeks burned. "As we said, we have no more information for you at this point, and I wish it was different. I've been there, Mrs. Cambridge. My own brother, I—"

"It's not *your* brother, though, Lei. It's *our* daughter, and you might be able to empathize, but we're not sure your organization can. We know what's happened. Can feel it in our bones. You want to give us a fucking resolution? Catch the bastard! Fuck me sideways. A bit of respect is all we want. A bit of dignity." She broke down again.

Colin threw an arm around her. "You'd better go."

Coghlan beat her down the stairs, but Nguyen waited until they were both in the squad car before she spoke up. "You stupid fucking idiot. I told you to let me do the talking."

"Just trying to help, Lei. Jesus."

"It's hard enough sitting on the fact we found blood at the scene without pissing them off. Next time, just look sad and let me do the human bit for Christ's sake."

He turned on the ignition. "Come on, my shout for coffee," he said. "Might make me feel a bit more human." He winked at Nguyen.

She turned away and watched Debbie cry as they reversed out of the property.

As the thin needle of shade supplied by the ancient telephone pole spiraled around the splintered post and dialed away the day, Katy shuffled with it, avoiding the bullshit sun. She was beginning to regret not accepting Maude's offer of a sandwich and a cold drink. It wouldn't have been so bad. Sure, she'd have had to have risked being introduced to the old duck's sons and nephews, but in retrospect, she'd probably have been able to sweet-talk her way into a lift to the next town. Nevertheless, she hadn't, and she had to wait for someone, anyone, to drive past and take a chance on picking up a hitchhiker. So far, people had been all too willing to help her out, meaning, essentially, things had been as she'd expected. The people had been lovely and given the recent news stories doing the rounds in this part of the state, none of them had liked to see a young girl like her hitching.

Bruised clouds promised a storm on the horizon, and they'd done a good job of ensuring the locals had stayed home. She wasn't ready to start walking yet, though. The sun would blast her into nothingness in no time if she tried, and if there was one thing she was sick of in the Outback, it was sunburn. Resigned, she wiped the sweat from her brow and waved another fly away from her face. There were probably seventeen more on her shoulder-blades, but whatever, they weren't biting ones, and fighting them off was a losing battle, at least until the rains came.

She was about to get her diary out to record her conversation with Maude when she heard the distinctive sound of a motorbike. Just her luck. When a vehicle did come along, it was one she probably wouldn't be able to squeeze into. Bugger.

She pricked her ears as it came closer. Above the whining engine—and the droning fly-song—a peal of thunder rolled in the distant clouds. As it echoed into nothingness, the bike appeared, a pinprick of motion on the horizon. Beggars couldn't be choosers out here with a storm brewing and Katy needed to get to the Bruce Highway so she could get further north. She popped her diary into her backpack and stepped into the blaring sun. Highway mirages glittered on the road as she stepped towards it. She used one hand to shield her eyes from the glaring sun and the other to stick her thumb out.

The rider slowed as he approached. Behind his black helmet, his face was indiscernible, but he had an electric guitar slung over his back, no case. He could have been a musical wasteland wanderer, but it didn't matter. There was space on the bike, and more importantly, the dude had a spare helmet strapped to the sissy bar. He flipped his visor up, revealing a young face with wispy hair. No doubt it tapered into a scrappy goatee. His eyes were hidden behind dark aviators.

"You shouldn't be hitching out here."

Shit, was he going to lecture her as well? That was the last thing she needed. At least on a motorbike, the chances for chit-chat would be minimal. "Yeah, the storm, I know. Sorry."

"Haven't you seen the papers? The storm's the least of your worries."

Again, bloody hell. With folks out here harping on about it, there was no wonder people in the cities figured the place was full of serial killers and drifters. "Not the papers," she said, sighing, "but I've heard."

He licked his lips. "Where you going? Highway? I'm going through to Brissie. Won't do to take you all the way, but I can get you to shelter."

"Bruce Highway's good. I'm going north from there."

The guy on the bike paused thoughtfully, shuffled, trying to see if there was room. "It's not ideal, but you'd better get on. Can't leave you out here."

"What, with a madman on the loose?"

He grinned. "Nah, with the storm coming."

"You sure?" She grinned at him, toying with him. "How do I know you're not the one who kidnapped those people?"

He took his glasses off. "Well, you wanna take your chances with the weather and whoever else is gonna offer you a ride on a day like this, you're more than welcome. It's gonna piss down, though. Might be hail from the look of the sky."

She made a performance of inspecting the clouds. "All right, but no funny business. And if you kill me, I guarantee I will get so much of your DNA under my fingernails they'll find you in seconds."

"Come on. Day's wasting." He scooted forward and waited for her to strap the helmet on. It smelled of dry, dusty garages and stale sweat. She pushed it down over her head and threw her leg over the bike. "Don't mind Old Suzie. She's coming all the way with me, and you're gonna have to try not to let her knock you as we ride."

"Suzie?"

"My guitar."

"Rightio then."

"You don't sound impressed."

He didn't realize it, but this bloke was going to make a fine entry in her book. "You can tell me all about it later," she said. "By the way, I'm Katy."

"Kip." Kip flipped his visor shut, revved the engine with a flourish and veered onto the road.

By the time Kip's EL250 had travelled two-hundred kilometers of highway, the sky had melted into a purple dusk, and Katy's arse was sore from the relentless vibration of the rough road. She felt like he'd managed to hit every pothole and bump on the Capricorn Highway, and when the service station appeared in the distance, she couldn't wait to stretch her legs.

As he pulled into the driveway, the first thumb-sized drops of rain spattered around them. The dry dusty scent of the Central Queensland plains and scrub forest mingled with the ozone and splashing rain to produce a pleasing aroma. She was taking it in, breathing deeply when Kip spoke for the first time since their initial meeting.

"I love that smell."

"Petrichor? It's amazing."

He looked at her as if she was mad. "Nah, not the petrol. The rain smell. You get it right when the rain first starts."

He wasn't the sharpest tool in the shed, but then she supposed he hadn't had the chance to go to university like she had. "Yeah, it's called petrichor. *Pet-ree-kor*." She enunciated it clearly, teasing him as she did so.

"Yeah, whatever you reckon. One of them fancy-pants words you don't need, is it?"

A word she didn't need? She'd never considered the possibility. "It's a word!"

"Yeah, but when are you gonna use it apart from when you wanna sound clever. Just say 'fresh rain smell.'"

She shook her head, wondering if he felt the same about whatever tricks he would like to pull on his guitar, and read the signs in the service station window. "Come on, I'll shout you a feed. It's the least I can do."

"All right. Let me fill her up and I'll join you."

The service station was about as stock-standard as one could be. An outdoor play area sprawled beneath weathered shade cloth, a small al fresco smoking area consisting of one small umbrella and a couple of scungy plastic tables sat beside the dunnies, and firewood, gas-canisters, and a large icebox finished the exterior features. She made her way across the refueling area, pausing briefly to let a blue Ford four-wheel-drive pass by. The driver ogled her, and she smiled awkwardly when he raised a finger in the universal gesture of greeting on country roads.

As the vehicle disappeared into the parking area, she shuddered. There was something off-putting about the guy behind the wheel. She tried not to be judgmental; had made it her reason for going bush to start with, but some people were creepy, plain and simple.

Inside, the service station was like most of the big ones she'd seen on the highways crisscrossing the state. The petrol counter sat on one side of the building, while the hotbox and café stretched out across the opposite side. The whole interior of the building smelled like warm cooking oil. She made straight for the hotbox and selected a bunch of greasy items she'd regret later: a lasagna topper, a couple of dim sums, a bucket of potato gems, two Chiko Rolls, and a deep-fried kabana. She ordered a couple of flat whites to go with the feast and took a seat at one of the plastic tables provided for those who wanted to sit and eat.

She knelt on the bench, not wanting to put any weight on her ass-cheeks if she didn't have to. If Kip was going all the way to Brisbane, he was probably going to need at least a week to stand when he got there. Even when they made it to the Bruce Highway, he was going to have half a day's travel to complete.

The sliding doors opened, and Kip entered. He had a bright green Mohawk and an anarchy symbol tattooed on the left side of his head. She grinned and waved him over. As he came, the skies opened. The rain fell hard, drowning out the industrial sounds bleeding over the counter from the kitchen and through the dusty screen-door behind it.

Droplets, blown by the gusting wind, splashed the windows, and her view of the outside world became dappled and obscure. "Made it just in time," she said.

He snorted. "That's set in and I've gotta be there by morning. Hopefully old Suzie's wires won't be too badly affected."

"Can a guitar get wet?"

"Won't be the first time. She's had more repairs than a bloody hire-car. It's what makes her punk."

Katy let the comment slide. She wasn't quite sure letting your guitar get wet was an act of rebellion, but she chose to assume he was referring to a DIY approach to maintenance and moved on. "Here, hope you like day-old hotbox food."

"Are you kidding? Lasagna toppers are legit the tits."

"The what?"

His face reddened. "Sorry."

She laughed. "I wasn't offended; just hadn't heard it before." She pushed the lasagna topper in his direction. "So you're in a band?"

"As of tomorrow. It's why I'm heading to Brissie."

"Bullshit." Here was a story she hadn't expected to get for her book, but she had to admit, it certainly fit the narrative she'd already figured out when it came to missing people like, well, like the ones the papers were worried about.

"Nah, fair dinkum."

The shit-eating grin meant he could only be telling the truth. "Go on."

He finished chewing his mouthful of lasagna topper and sipped his coffee. "I'll give you the short version. I'd rather find out what you're doing out here in the sticks."

"You first."

"Do you know the band Primordial Effigy?"

"Nope." She guessed not many people did.

Kip looked bummed. "Their guitarist's leaving, and I'm the replacement."

"Piss off. *Really?*"

"Really. They were up here for a festival in Longreach: one of those radio-station specials they put on for country towns with nothing else going on and their guitarist got too fucked-up on cheap beer to play. They asked if anyone knew how to play their songs and I was like 'hello'. Once they'd seen me play a couple of 'em, they told me I was getting on stage with them."

"You're a bloody hero. All of Longreach relying on you to save the day and there you are. You got a cape in your backpack somewhere? Sure you don't need to put your undies on the outside?"

"Ah, stop it. They're pretty easy: all open chords and palm-muted riffs."

She nodded as if she knew what he meant. "And now you're in the band for good?"

"Well, it wasn't quite so simple, but yeah. They kept in touch and made sure I was keen. They knew Trent, their previous guitarist, was leaving to sort his dramas with the booze out and they reckoned I deserved a chance. I've been back and forward a few times to play small gigs, and this time I'm staying for good."

She pulled her diary out of her bag. "You mind if I take some notes? This is a great story."

He scrunched his face, confused.

"Don't worry, it's nothing bad. I'm writing a book about the people you meet in the Outback. My granddad was from out this way, and he always said people out here never got a fair go because everyone thought they were a bunch of rednecks. Now I've finished my degree, I'm getting straight to business and putting a manuscript together. It's gonna be a series of essays on the different people out here, and I reckon you'd be great to include."

A huge peal of thunder rumbled overhead. The lights flickered and then steadied. She'd almost forgotten the storm amid the chat, but the realization she'd have been stuck out in it without Kip hit home. "Hey, thanks for picking me up. Wouldn't have blamed you for driving straight past."

"Nah, I told you, there's a fucken maniac out here somewhere. Three people—our age, a bit younger maybe—have gone missing in the last few months. I couldn't have left you there if I wanted to."

She finished her Chiko Roll and pursed her lips, considering whether she should push the next line of questioning before going ahead with it. "This is it, though, right: the reason for the book. You don't think it's possible those kids left of their own free will—like you are?"

"Nah, they'd have told someone. Look at me, my mate Gus knows all the details. Even told me not to ride a stupid motorbike all the way to Brissie."

"What if their home life was shit?"

"They'd have told *someone*. In this case, no one knows where the fuck they are, and there's a few people saying there's a serial killer out here. Reckon the missing rich girl from a couple of weeks ago is the latest."

"But you don't reckon the myths and rumors start because kids might leave of their own accord. You know, two or three kids bail without saying a word, and you know, Bob's your uncle."

Guffaws burst out from the table behind them. Katy turned to see the driver of the blue Ford standing unnervingly close. "Now you're supposed to say, 'And if you cut off his bollocks, he'd be your auntie!'"

Up close, the guy gave off dodgier vibes than he did when she'd first seen him. His skin was pale and clammy, marked by unnatural craters and ridges. His thin hair fell over spectacles bearing the smudges of greasy fingers. He stunk to high heaven, smelling like he'd been rolling in carrion; like he'd bathed in roadkill. His eyes were dark and small behind the glasses. A vein twitched in his neck and a fly sat rubbing its forelegs together on his brow. Literally nothing about him felt right.

THREE

HE STEPPED CLOSER to their table and gestured for them to make room. Thankfully, he didn't take the seat directly beside Katy, but he did spin a chair across from a nearby table and assume a position trapping them in their booth. Thankfully, the fly previously sitting on his brow had taken to the air, but his rank breath drifted across the table. Katy pushed the remains of her kabana away.

He reached for it, snatched it, and popped it into his mouth. Before he'd finished chewing, he pointed to Kip. "Here to see the craters, are you? Have to say, you'll struggle on a pissweak bike like the one you rode in on. Piece of shit, if I do say so."

Katy caught Kip's *what should I say* glance but couldn't think of any way to help him. The fly had buzzed back and perched on the man's cheek. He didn't seem at all fazed by it and continued to wait for an answer as he munched on the kabana. As he chewed, something else seemed to move in his face. Katy couldn't tell whether it was a weird nervous twitch, but it looked like something sliding, burrowing, beneath his skin. She fought the urge to gag and shrugged her shoulders at Kip.

"Look, mate," Kip said, sliding the greasy paper bags the food had come in away from the strange visitor, "we're trying to eat our tucker. Do you mind?"

There was a sudden pause in the drumming of the rain, and then it came down again, harder than before. The guy reclined, startling his pet fly into take-off and raised both hands so they could see his open palms. "Don't get your bloody knickers in a knot. I'm only making friends. Was gonna offer to show you around."

"Yeah, thanks," Katy said, "but we want to eat and get a move on. We were kinda in the middle of a conversation, so if we could get some privacy, we'd appreciate it."

The guy's mouth dropped. His black teeth demonstrated exactly why his breath reeked. "You're trying to tell me you don't wanna see the craters. They're fucken legendary. Literally made by meteors from outer space and you wanna forego the opportunity. Fuck me sideways, you kids are weird today."

Kip kneaded his temples before speaking. "Mate, you might not know this, but they're not real impact craters. It's a myth. They're from volcanic activity, and if we did want to see them, I don't think we'd go for a tour with the first random bloke to hassle us about them in a truck-stop servo."

Katy cheered inwardly. Decided to chip in and present a united front. "Yeah, no offense, but it'd be good if you'd leave us alone."

The guy smashed his fist down on the table, sending plastic cutlery bouncing and coffee sloshing. "You don't know shit from clay, mate! Those fucken CSIRO wankers are telling you what the government wants 'em to. Besides, you're not going anywhere more important than the sights of this bewdiful place."

"Please, piss off. I don't want to get the manager to call security," Katy said.

"Nah, let us know, fuckya. I'll give you directions; make sure you get to see some sights on the way out. Shit you won't find in those tourist maps the authorities print."

"Really?" Kip asked. "Really?"

The man's face glitched into something far more serious. More dangerous. "There's a fly on your grub."

"What?" Kip asked.

Katy looked down. There was a fly there. And it wasn't the one crawling on his face.

"You know, fucking buzz buzz, shit on your dinner, maggots in your eyeballs. A fly. You know, a fucking fly. Like this one." He pointed to the fly on his face and glared.

The rain pissed down, slashing the windows and leaving cutting runnels on the glass. Katy stood. "Okay, we're done. Fuck off and leave us alone before I call the cops."

He laughed. Huge booming guffaws. "You think the pigs are gonna bring their pretty little cars out onto these black roads on this deadly night do you, girlie?"

Katy looked nervously to the counter, but the girl was busy mopping the tiles near the entrance. "Leave us alone," she said, shuddering.

The man snapped his attention onto Kip. With lightning speed, his hand shot out and snatched the fly from his face. It buzzed and pulsed between his thumb and forefinger, but it was going nowhere. "He fucken comes over, crawls on my face, and wants to get away. Cheeky as you like, right?"

Kip leaned as far away from the man as possible. Katy followed his lead.

"Nah, nah, nah-nah-nah," the guy said. "You pay attention. This is important." He held the fly, which continued buzzing erratically, right in front of Kip's terrified face. "They've got thousands of eyes, these bastards."

With sleight of hand, he spun his fingers, and when they were still again, he had the fly by its two delicate wings.

"Don't," Katy said.

"Like I said, thousands of eyes." He ripped out its wings. "He's got no bloody wings though!" He exploded into loud, barking laughter, guffawing so aggressively even the rain seemed to stop and listen.

"You should go," Katy said.

"Hang on, first you've gotta tell me what you call a fly with no wings."

She looked at him. At Kip. Back to him.

"Go on then, it's a piece of piss this one." He drummed his fingers impatiently, his cheek bulging as if something was moving beneath it. "Come on! My mum could get it right and she's fucken dead!" He laughed again, not lifting his eyes from hers.

She took a deep breath.

"I'll give you a hint: it's the same thing you call a stupid cunt trying to get through the Outback without a ride." He waited, eyes blazing, then lost patience. "All right, fucken give up, then. It's a walk. Get it? It's gotta walk everywhere so you can't call it a fucken fly unless you're a liar. You know, like someone who makes shit up about the craters. Like the people who don't want you to know the terrifying truth."

She wondered if she could push past him; if he'd let her.

"Seriously, though, I'll prove those craters aren't volcanic. Load of shit, that is."

Whatever had been sliding around beneath his cheek had moved. The bulge wriggled under the flesh beneath his earlobe. Katy found herself transfixed by it.

"Now, you," he said, resting his elbow on the table and pointing aggressively at Kip, "Where the fuck are you riding a little pansy motorbike with a stupid haircut like that?" His eyes had narrowed, and a steely edge had crept into his voice.

"It's none of your business," Katy said before Kip could answer. Every reptilian fiber of her body was screaming. This guy was more than scary, he was dangerous, and if she could, she'd have run a mile.

"I wasn't talking to you, city girl. You've got tourist from the big smoke written all over you, but this little prick's got runaway scrawled on his forehead." He turned to Kip, prodding the air with his extended finger. "What is it then, cunt; where are you going?"

"Brissie. I'm going to fucken Brissie okay."

"Christ. That's a long way . . . Your arse must be able to take a righteous pounding. So . . . *who's expecting you?*"

The waitress approached. "Everything okay here?" She inspected the three of them as she grabbed their scraps. Returning to the kitchen, she pivoted and spoke again. "You might wanna consider hitting the road again soon if you're not going into the motel. Rain's only gonna get heavier. Some of the creeks'll break their banks in another hour or two."

"Yeah, we were about to hit the road," Kip said.

"You didn't answer my question," the strange guy said. "Who's expecting you?"

"Fucking everyone," Kip said. "My parents, my bandmates, and everyone else down there. They're gonna throw me a big fucken party."

"Wasn't so hard, was it?"

"Now, excuse us will you. We were in the middle of something."

He grinned, raised his hands as if he meant no harm. "Well, I'll be seeing you round," the guy said. "You can be sure of it."

"God, I hope not," Katy said.

The big guy grimaced at her in what she figured was supposed to be a smile. "All right, I'll go then. Wouldn't wanna get trapped by rising water, would I?" He leered as he left, and rain rushed through the sliding door, wetting the linoleum floor as he exited the servo. They watched in silence as he drove out of the car-park and onto the road, heading in the direction of the Bruce Highway.

"What the fuck?" Katy asked. She suppressed a shudder as she remembered some of the finer points of the discussion.

"One for your book," Kip said.

"I'm rethinking it after meeting him. What a weirdo."

Kip smiled. "I'm sure he's just eccentric. You gonna crash here or you gonna come with me. I've gotta get to the Bruce tonight. Need to be in Brisbane in the morning."

"I'll come," she said. "Last thing I need is for him to come through here and find me in the motel." Kip's claim the guy was probably an eccentric rattled through her head. If there was such a thing as an extremely dangerous bloke out here, old mate fit the bill. Not only because he was threatening, but because he was crazy. There was something very, very troubling about him, and she didn't want to ever see him again.

As Kip sidled the bike to the slip-road, a huge semi-trailer juggernauted past, headlights driving forward into the pounding rain. It hit a pool of greasy water and an arterial spray of grit and run-off sloshed in a fanned arc, engulfing them and splashing onto the cracked tarmac. Katy wiped her visor and shivered. She'd bemoaned the heat earlier, but she would enjoy this leg of the ride a whole lot less.

Kip let the water clear from the slip-lane and then steered the 250 onto the dark road. At times, she felt like he was the only one keeping to the speed limit. Every other vehicle swooped past them at high speed, spraying water onto their faces. She realized Kip wanted to go faster but the bike was maxed out.

When the vehicle behind them began to tailgate, high beams glaring, she wondered what the driver's problem was.

Kip pulled onto the road shoulder to let them pass, but instead of going around, the car stayed close, its high beams stabbing into the dark night, casting everything before them in vivid relief and obscuring everything between them and the car in dazzling white light.

Kip came to a complete stop, and the car did the same. When the driver stepped out of the vehicle and into the blinding light in front of the right-hand lamp, his silhouette was unmistakable.

"Fucking go," she said. "It's him. It's him!"

Kip spun his head round. "What the fuck does he want?"

She pounded her palm on his shoulder. "Go!"

Kip revved the throttle. The guy jumped into his car.

As the bike lurched forward, it felt slower than ever. It was like the dream she always had where her desperate punch lacked the conviction or power to have any impact. As the tachometer tickled the red line of the gauge, the speedometer could only climb slowly behind it.

The car, the same blue vehicle she'd seen at the servo, closed the distance with ease. The engine roared, making short work of the distance Kip's EL250 had labored over. If she could have seen beyond the glaring brightness thrown out by the headlamps, she'd have seen the fucking weirdo inside laughing or licking his lips or clutching the steering wheel with white knuckles and a look of berserk intensity on his pockmarked face.

He revved the vehicle into touching distance and hit the horn. The sound was immense, engulfing Katy in a wash of angry noise. A car in the opposite lane flashed its high beams, reminding their pursuer to kill his own, but he didn't relent. He moved closer. Blasted the horn again.

Kip veered the bike into the safety lane. Grit and gravel kicked up from the wheel, but if he thought he was going to drop behind the pursuing vehicle he was mistaken. The crazy bastard swerved right in behind them. Kip gunned the accelerator again, not wanting his rear wheel chewed beneath the Ford's grill.

The bike jumped forward, the engine moaning with the effort and Katy felt sorry for ever volunteering to ride with him; for slowing him down.

The huge engine roared and the light behind them disappeared. The Ford swept around them in a dramatic maneuver. Seconds later, it was in front of them, its brake lights glowing red.

Kip pumped his own brakes, but it was hopeless. The 250 skidded and she felt herself leaving the seat. She let go of the sissy bar as she tried to protect her face, and then she felt the crunch of metal. She rolled over the Ford and slipped down its bonnet where she lay on the ground. Dimly, she was aware of Kip flying farther; of the bike rolling into the bushes beside the road and of Kip screaming in pain.

The driver-side door of the vehicle opened and slammed shut, and next thing she knew, the man stood over her. He prodded her with the toe of his boot, and when she only groaned, he grunted and forged on towards Kip, who was screaming in agony against a "CAUTION: KANGAROOS" sign.

"I'm glad you stopped," the guy said. "Got some things I wanna show you."

Kip tried to scramble away. He pressed down on his elbow and screamed again. He was in deep shit. Katy forced herself to her feet and tried to mount a futile run. She staggered, wobbling, and shoved the guy. "Fuck off," she told him as he blurred into two identical men.

He shot out a hand, grabbing her by the throat. He used his free hand to flick up her visor. "I'll deal with you in a minute." He threw her to the ground and kicked her hard in the back. "Fucking stay there."

She doubled over. Tears welled in her eyes, and she could only watch as he hefted Kip by the strap of his motorcycle helmet.

"Will you quit fucking crying?" he asked. "No one's gonna hear you." He drew a knife from a sheath on his belt. Katy screamed.

"Relax," he said. "I'm not gonna fucking hurt him. Not here." He cut the strap and yanked the helmet free. As Kip dropped to his knees, clutching his elbow, the man felt the helmet's weight with a curious motion of his hands and then swung it down, cracking it into Kip's face like a sledgehammer.

Kip, flattened by the blow, sprawled. His head crunched onto the gravel. Blood poured from his nose. The man laughed.

He grabbed Kip by the foot and dragged him towards the four-wheel-drive.

Katy climbed to her feet, using the road barrier as a crutch. She scrambled over it, falling on the other side and crawled towards the bushes.

"Where do you think you're going, sweetheart? You've got some sightseeing to do as well; you can't be running off on me." He grasped her shirt and lifted her to her feet with an easy movement.

She screamed.

He laughed. "Like I told your boyfriend, no one's gonna hear you out here. Watch," he said, putting one hand beside his mouth as if to guide a shout. "HELP!" he screamed. "HELP!" He laughed again. "See, nothing."

She struggled, throwing an elbow at him as he dragged her. It must have caught him because his grip loosened, and then she felt a boot in her arse. The force of the kick pushed her forward onto her knees and he wrestled her helmet from her. Once he had it free, his meaty palm shot out. The wallop rang loud in her ears, and she hit the deck.

FOUR

THUNDER RUMBLED OVERHEAD, and gloomy daylight leaked in through rusted-out cracks and punctures in the roof above her. These weak spotlights lit motes of dust. The droning hum of flies buzzed loudly around her. Hundreds of them careened through the glowing streaks of light, but none caught her attention as much as the huge one sitting deathly still on the ceiling directly above her. It had to be as large as a mouse, and even from her prone position, she could make out individual hairs on its abdomen. She blinked, hoping for it to disappear. It didn't. It only sat and watched the other flies crawling on her.

Her hands were tied, so she couldn't swat them away, and when she screamed, she realized her jaws were held open by some sort of mechanism. The sound ignited movement in her mouth. Things crawled around in there, inspecting her flesh, probably burrowing inside her.

The buzzing swelled in volume as the flies all around zizzed past her, creating their own tiny rushes of wind. Several landed on her privates. Her legs were tied open, and from the feeling of motion down there, she had lost her pants. God, no. No. *No.*

Her cheek throbbed, her back ached, and she felt sick. She had to get to grips with her situation, had to look for a way out. "Kip?" she tried to ask. She couldn't form words properly. Whatever was holding her mouth open felt hooked and rigid; wouldn't let her formulate the shapes she needed to enunciate properly.

She breathed deep. Something buzzed in her nostril, and she snorted, trying to dislodge it. A fly shot out, droned, and landed on her eyebrow.

Meat hooks hung above her, some with strips of meat dangling from them. Putrefaction filled the air. Miasmic gases and the stench of old blood and rotten flesh ghosted around the room. She realized how wrong she'd been. Something terrible had happened here. Those girls hadn't run away; the boy probably hadn't either.

Approaching footsteps squelched on wet ground outside and then the door slammed open, letting more light into the room. In the corner of her eye, a meaty palm pulled a string. A fluorescent light flickered and clicked on, adding its own buzzing to the ever-present drone of the flies. "Morning, love."

The guy from the service station loomed over her. Flies crawled across him and in this light, she could see he was pale and sick. More than one thing burrowed beneath his skin. A drop of greasy sweat ran down his forehead and splashed onto her cheek, once again sending flies skittering.

"Now, I know what you're thinking, but you've gotta know I haven't touched you . . . you know, down there. Not my place. I had to check if you were . . . a virgin. You are, aren't you? Didn't think city sluts like you could be, but . . . "

She moaned; tried to tell him to take whatever was lodging her mouth open out of her face.

"I know what you want, and I need to know, so listen close: no fucken squealing or else there'll be trouble. It's kinda picky and it needs a good girl." He reached for one of the hooks. "You promise to be good. One grunt for yes, two grunts for no."

She grunted once.

He unhooked her mouth, and she screamed.

He immediately pinched her nose shut and clasped a hand over her mouth.

She thrashed, but he didn't relent.

"I *told you* to be good."

Her lungs burned and as she gasped, she was sure she could feel flies going down her throat. She coughed, certain they were in her airways, buzzing, exploring.

"Are you stupid enough to scream again?"

She grunted.

"You are?"

Her heart beat faster. Her lungs contracted.

"Remember, I need two grunts for no, so let me ask: are you stupid enough to scream again?"

She grunted twice.

He released her nostrils, and she sucked as much air through them as she could.

"I'm serious, love. No screaming. You got me?"

She grunted.

He released her mouth. "I need to know. *It* needs to know. You a virgin, girlie?"

She wasn't sure how to answer. Either response could be wrong. It could be what he wanted. It could be his kink. On the other side of the coin, it could be the thing he didn't want. It could mean death, and she hated him for it. She'd come out here to prove her grandpa was right, and this evil bastard had shattered her world, shattered his truths, and he did not deserve to know her secrets.

"The truth, girlie. You ain't for me, don't worry."

She nodded, realizing whatever this "It" he kept referring to might be, it was the only thing keeping her alive. "Yes," she said. "Yes."

"Good. Mary was a virgin, and the mother of God can only deliver Him through an immaculate conception. That's you, girlie. You're Mary, and you're gonna have a baby. You're gonna see the craters, and you're gonna have a baby."

With every word, she felt herself wanting to curl into a ball and cry. She couldn't. She'd read enough true crime to know she had to keep her cool, had to wait for her chance to escape, had to stay strong and refuse to die, just like Joanne Lees. "No," she said. "I can't. I'm only young. I'm not ready yet."

"You don't have a say in the matter." He re-clamped her mouth and disappeared from view again. He rummaged on a nearby bench and when he returned, he held conical pliers for her to see. "This is gonna hurt, but I promise you it'll be worth it."

He reached into her mouth and clamped them over one of her teeth.

The huge fly on the ceiling watched.

Kip heard the screaming from his own precarious position. He could rotate his head to look in her direction, but he was gagged and could only offer muffled screams in response. He was tied upright to a large square of ribbed-steel reinforcing mesh in a Jesus Christ pose. His face was swollen and bruised. His congested nose hurt. His ankles were crossed, and masking tape held his feet, waist, and arms to the steel. His elbow, obviously broken, hurt like a motherfucker and the pain washed through him, leaving him nauseous.

As bad as he had it, though, Katy had it worse. He hated to think what was happening to her in there and couldn't believe things had come to this. He should have arrived in Albion. Should have met with the boys in Primordial Effigy; shared a billy with them for the first time as a band member; strummed his guitar and whacked out some riffs as Pete smashed his drums and Dan belted out some angry vocals while thumping his bass strings like a man possessed. Thankfully he hadn't been lying when he'd told the weird bastard at the servo people were expecting him. If the boys hadn't called the cops already, they would soon, for sure.

But, if the cops *were* going to rescue him, they couldn't come soon enough. Not only was this place already filling with the rainwater leaking through the rusted tin roof, but it was full of the biggest black flies he'd ever seen. They zigzagged through the room like atoms, crashing into each other and veering off in different paths. Worse, he was sure the jars he could make out on the dimly lit shelves were full of rotten meat and maggots.

He tried to call through his gag again. He hated to think why Katy was no longer calling out; why she had stopped screaming in pain.

The interior door burst open, clattered against a milk crate full of junk, and swung shut in juddering lurches. He thought he caught a glimpse of Katy lying prone, tied to something, but the view was so momentary he couldn't be certain.

The big fella walked in. He hadn't changed out of the clothes he wore yesterday. He was in the same blue polo shirt, navy blue footy shorts, and leather boots.

Kip moaned again.

The big guy grinned. "Hold your horses, mate. I'm coming. Jesus fuck." As he approached, he pulled a Bowie knife from one of the shelves and unsheathed it. "We'd better have a look at your arm. Can't have it getting infected, can we?"

Kip shook his head. The last thing he wanted was this guy going anywhere near it.

The guy flicked it with a thick, stubby finger.

Pain erupted. Synapses exploded in Kip's skull, causing him to scream. He'd never felt anything like it in his life; not even the moment of impact when he'd landed on it last night.

"Hurts, does it? Better give us a squiz." The guy cut through the tape with the blade, not worrying about the pressure or whether he was catching flesh beneath it.

Kip vomited behind his gag.

"Mate," the bloke said. "You're gonna bloody choke yourself." He pulled the gag down and the puke slid down the front of Kip's shirt. Flies buzzed over to the fresh waste, landed on him, splashed in it. "Seriously, mate, we've got shit to do, so hold onto your lunch. You're fasting, and you're gonna need all the energy you can muster." He scooped a handful of the spew and forced it into Kip's mouth.

Kip spat it out.

"Maaaate." He scooped it up again, popped it in Kip's gob and clamped a hand over his mouth and nostrils. "Fucken swallow, mate. You need your sustenance."

Tears welled in Kip's eyes and the man became a pale blur.

He turned his attention to Kip's elbow. "Christ! Looks like a dog's breakfast!" He yanked the arm, and if Kip thought the previous pain was bad, it was nothing compared to this latest bout of agony. He screamed and in response, he thought he heard a muffled shout come from the room where Katy was being kept.

"Your girlfriend's all right. She's gonna need to be. She's chosen. Gonna have a baby after she sees the craters. You too. You're gonna be parents together."

Kip shook his head. What the fuck was this guy talking about?

"Not what you think. Anyway, not important. Can't have you going out there with an infected arm. We'd better fix it up." He went to the shelves and retrieved one of the jars.

As Kip had expected, it was full of wriggling maggots and buzzing flies. His eyes went wide, and he shook his head in desperation.

"Now, I was going to cut you to show you this, but then the whole compound fracture thing happened so I thought I mightn't have to. The thing is, *I really want to*." He jammed the knife into Kip's elbow.

Kip screamed again.

The man twisted the knife as if it were a screwdriver then pushed it down to bone before levering it out. Blood welled and dripped to the floor. "I bet you didn't know flies are fucken grouse at healing shit? Well, their larvae are. Maggots are." The lunatic poured a handful of maggots into the palm of his hand, lifted the bleeding flap of skin on Kip's arm and lovingly placed them underneath it. "You'll be amazed at the results."

Kip tried to shake them free.

"They're there for your benefit, you silly bastard. Stop being a baby. Like I told you, you're going to need your strength for later."

Kip let his head drop, resting his chin on his collarbone. He couldn't help but hope for a reprieve; hope his friends in Brissie had called the cops and had told them to be on the lookout for an abandoned EL250 on the side of the Capricorn Highway. If he refused to believe they'd called, he had no reason to think he could escape. If he couldn't escape, then he really was the failure he'd always feared.

Lei spun away from her own desk, a fastidious set-up with childhood photos of her with her family and her missing twin brother, Pham. Charged, she kicked Coghlan's office chair, interrupting his call, and slung her bag over her shoulder.

Coghlan spun around, pissed, holding the phone between his chin and his shoulder. "Hold on," he said to his wife on the other end of the call. "What the fuck is so important?"

"We've gotta go," she said. "Tell Hails I apologize for interrupting, but we've got a call we've gotta chase up. Abandoned motorbike on the Landsborough. Engine's warm and we need to move. Could be a lead. I'll tell you the rest on the way."

Coghlan shook his head and turned to his desk. "All right, hun, I take it you caught that?" He flipped Nguyen the bird. "Love you too, hun. Keep an eye on the creek and call me if it reaches the driveway. Experts think it's gonna be raging by the morning. If it rises sooner, call the office and I'll blow this joint."

"Let's go, Chase, come on."

"Yeah, Lei says hi." He looked at his partner. "Hailey says g'day."

As she pulled a raincoat over her uniform, she remembered herself. "How you going, Hailey. I'll bring him home safe; I promise."

"Okay, babe, give the girls kisses and tell 'em I love 'em." He replaced the phone. "And you wonder why she hates your guts," he said. "She's supposed to the one busting my balls, not you."

Nguyen laughed. "The more of us busting your balls the better. You need it." She threw him the keys and pointed at his umbrella. "You're gonna need that too."

When they reached the Pajero, she pulled her pad out of her bag. "Not far east of the big servo."

"So, why's this so urgent? Not like the engine's gonna be warm when we get there; not in this delightful weather."

"Because we had another phone call. Turns out a young bloke should have made it to Brissie by now. And guess what he was travelling on . . . "

Coghlan turned the key. "Rightio, tell me the details as I drive." He pulled out of the car-park, whacked on the police lights so he could drive as fast as he wanted, and slammed the accelerator. "So who's the kid?"

FIVE

PASTRONI CLOSED THE door on Kip and let his focus drift across to Mother. Her eye sockets, empty but for the flies and maggots crawling through and across her desiccated flesh, stared beyond him. Wherever it was she watched from, she could see him performing God's work.

Her corpse was propped by straps he'd hung from the ceiling and her hands were clasped in eternal prayer thanks to loops of wire he'd tied around them. He approached and knelt before it, taking in the contours of her wasted skin. The aromas of her bodily presence dissipated into the heavens, and he inhaled them as he made the sign of the cross. She'd always told him to do it once before prayer and once after if he wanted God to listen. To him, it wasn't necessarily true, but it was a habit he wouldn't break. It would be disrespectful when she'd done so much for him. It had been her who'd first taken him out to the morass, shown him the black water and the flies calling it home, and whispered to him of the God brought here by the meteors.

He crossed himself yet again. "This time, Mum. This time we've got the right ones. I swear."

The flies took to the air, hovered, and buzzed in harmony. They coalesced into a cloud around her, giving her the form of a swirling black angel. It stretched a rippling arm of flies across to brush his cheek; to cradle him.

Hands held in reverence he closed his eyes. He began to hum, taking two or three attempts to get the tone right, before harmonizing with the flies' own drone.

Maggots moved beneath his skin, and the undulating sensation beneath his epidermis became pronounced. The larvae of God, what most people thought of as maggots, wriggled towards the pockmarked breathing holes they'd chewed into his cheeks, his scalp, his flesh. They stuck their heads out and stretched their pearlescent bodies towards his mother's corpse. When they reached their fully extended length, they opened their mouths and produced the same humming as Pastroni himself.

He opened his eyes and waved his fingers at the humanoid cloud of flies beckoning him to come closer, to come and worship the God calling the morass home. He stared deep into his mother's empty eye sockets. In response the flies peeled away, unzipping the humanoid shape surrounding her. They alighted on her back, out of sight. The maggots beneath her own corrupt flesh found the airholes they had chewed into her, and they stretched forward, eager to meet the maggots stretching out of Pastroni's skin.

They stayed locked in position for moments and as the resonant drone of the hum vibrated through him, her dry and cracked lips began to move. It wasn't her voice pouring forth like black swamp-water, though. What he heard was the sound of God and it excited him. Soon, the Father would walk among them on Earth, and Pastroni would be his right-hand man, walking by his side as he rebuilt the world.

Despite the driving rain bouncing off her raincoat and the fact Coghlan had decided to wait in the car until she'd sussed out the lay of the land, Lei Nguyen couldn't help but feel excited. Sure, the prick who'd taken those last girls had struck again, but this time he'd fucked up. Previous abductions had been quick and clean; had left scant evidence. This, a damaged EL250, clearly marked with royal blue paint in a collision, had been hastily disposed of and left visible from the road. Somewhere, there would be a car with matching scrapes, and when they found it, they could start looping the noose for the motherfucker.

The door to their four-wheel-drive cracked open and an umbrella popped out. From beneath the percussive raindrops pounding it—and everything else—a gruff male voice called to her. "It's registered to a Kip Smith. Lives out near Longreach. Same kid the Brissie mob called in about. Call it in. Get forensics to come and suss it out, I reckon."

Fucking Coghlan was the laziest bastard she knew when it

came to this stuff. "Bust a move then," she said, pulling her hood tighter. "You've got the radio."

The umbrella disappeared and she returned her focus to the bike. She snapped a few shots with her phone. Already, the footprints she could see here were heavily eroded by the running rainwater. Rain speckled her phone-screen. If the kid had come from Longreach, he would have had to have fueled up along the road, and there weren't many service stations out here.

She pulled a glove over her hand and rapped a knuckle on the fuel-tank. Full. He must have done it recently. She dropped the phone in the pocket, stepped under the crime scene tape, and jogged to the passenger side of the car. "Head to the BP."

"You don't want something better than hotbox food?"

She shook her head, lips pursed. "Just fucking drive. He's put in petrol recently, which means he'll be on camera. Hopefully we can get a vehicle with matching paint there too."

"It's lunchtime; you don't want to do it after?"

For fuck's sake. She slapped the dashboard. "Now! Go! Shit, man!" Finding the bike had been too fucking easy. The guy had left no clues whatsoever before. It might mean nothing, but she couldn't shake the feeling it might mean a whole lot more.

Coghlan chuckled. "You're wasted out here in the sticks," he said. "This one might be your big break."

"It's not a movie, Chase. People's lives could be at stake, and if we can get him on camera, we might get his license plate. From there, well, you know what happens from there."

"You think the kids might be alive?"

She sat on it for a minute. They hadn't found any bodies yet. Until they did, there might be hope for them, just like there was for her twin brother. Sixteen years ago, he'd gone missing from a playground in the suburbs of Rockhampton. They'd never found him, and if she could find these kids, then maybe one day she could find him too.

"You all right?" Coghlan asked.

"I don't wanna take chances. Turn the siren on and fucking drive."

The bleary-eyed girl behind the counter watched them come in with complete disinterest. Nguyen approached, pulling her badge and identification.

"I saw the car," the girl said. "I know you're coppers."

"We were hoping you might be able to help us with something."

"Figured. Not like you fueled up."

Coghlan bristled. "We could've been coming for food," he said.

"No donuts here."

Nguyen laughed and put a hand out to stop Coghlan retaliating. Coghlan's monstrous gut spoke—and consumed—volumes. The girl was bang on the money, and besides, she had a cheeky grin which meant there was no harm in what she was saying. The locals out here liked to banter. They liked to give you shit, and if you got offended, you truly weren't one of them. With them, there were no pretenses. Nope, as long as you weren't a tall poppy and as long as you didn't talk incessantly, you were bloody golden in their eyes.

"So what do you need?" the girl asked.

"We were wondering if anyone came through here on a 250 motorbike last night. We know you probably saw a few bikes, but we're looking for one in particular."

"There was a couple on a bike. Dunno what sort it was, but he had a Mohawk. She was straight out of the city."

Nguyen looked at Coghlan, who dipped the image of Kip's license towards her. The kid had a Mohawk. "Two of them, you said?"

The girl nodded. "Yeah, they came and grabbed a feed right before the storm first started."

"Anyone else in around then?"

"One bloke," the girl said, leaning in towards Nguyen. "Fucking weirdo," she said. "He comes in here all the time. Talks to customers. He was really hassling these two last night."

"Those cameras work?" Coghlan asked, pointing to the CCTV cams in the corners of the ceiling.

"They're not painted on."

"Your boss won't mind if we have the footage?" Nguyen asked.

"Won't give a rat's ass," the girl said.

Nguyen nodded. "Okay, good, what can you tell us about this bloke? What's he drive?"

"Big blue Ranger. It'll be on camera too."

Nguyen couldn't believe her luck.

SIX

KATY HAD COME to think of him as the maggot-man and as she stirred, she couldn't help but be aware of his presence. He'd come in while she was drowsing. His labored breathing provided a counterpoint to the thunder and the steady drumming of the rain. She'd woken as soon as she'd heard it.

He stood in front of the sliding glass door and watched the outside area. From the steady dripping of the water through the leaky roof and the wet, moldy smell of decay hanging beneath the sweet smell of putrescence, she figured he must be watching the rain; watching the puddles grow.

"Won't be long," he said. "The smaller creeks burst their banks last night. Big ones are almost there. Then the rivers go."

She began to cry again. She didn't think she could have had any more tears, but whenever she thought she was running out of them, there always seemed to be a new supply. She moaned. Her mouth, already sore and chafed by the restraints he'd burdened her with, ached terribly from the amateur dental surgery the evil bastard had performed.

As her shoulders heaved, flies buzzed out of her mouth in a sickening wave of undulating chaos. Her belly lurched and as she gagged, she became aware the flies were no longer the only creatures moving around in her permanently open mouth. Things wriggled in there. She tried not to think about the fact they were maggots, but she couldn't help picturing them burrowing through the fleshy wounds he'd left when he pried her molars free. So far, the maggots had kept the welling blood from clogging her throat, but surely the infection was already rife within her; was rotting her from the inside-out.

"You heard me, then? Means you're doing well. You should be proud. When this is all done, you're gonna have a special place by

His side. You'll be venerated." He whistled, impressed with the possibility. "Deadset, you'll be the mother of the new world."

She screamed. For hours, she'd been waiting for a chance to get away, but the more time passed, the harder it was to keep her hopes up. When Bradley Murdoch had taken Joanne Lees, she'd escaped him then and there while he was fucking about with her boyfriend's dead body. If she was ever going to have a moment to seize, Katy had to keep her wits about her. The problem was the maggots. Them and the flies. They moved as if she was gargling them, making it hard to concentrate. A maggot plopped down her trachea. She coughed. More flies buzzed out of her mouth, and she choked down tears again. She wouldn't give him the satisfaction, even if she could feel her breath coming in rapid, hitching, gasps.

"Don't fucken panic," the guy said. He rested a heavy hand on her head. "I know it's all a shock, but I've gotta show you something. You've done better than all the rest and you've gotta make sure you don't give up."

If she could have shaken her head without the clamping hooks pulling against her pained maw, she would have. Instead, she tried to make pleading noises. Anything to make him think she would cooperate with him.

"I'm gonna loosen off your straps so we can talk," he said. "You know the deal: no screaming."

She grunted once.

He did as promised and lifted her head gently so she could see the room better. In the corner, an awkward pile of blankets was dumped haphazardly.

He propped her head with a cushion and made his way across to the pile. "As I said, you've done better than all the rest, but this'll be good motivation for you."

As he lifted the blanket, she closed her eyes, not wanting to see what was under there; not wanting confirmation. Her suspicions were enough, and with everything else conspiring to steal her hope, she didn't want to see the thing she'd been smelling since she first woke in this prison.

"Open your bloody eyes. You weren't first choice, you weren't, so you're gonna need to make sure It knows *you* were the *best choice*." He whipped the blanket with a flourish and flies exploded from beneath it. They buzzed around, making angry sounds and Katy's eyes settled on the corpse there.

The girl was young, probably younger than Katy, but it didn't matter, she was dead, and she'd died in only a single shoe. A pink Converse. Katy wondered if she was looking at her own future.

The man yanked the corpse by one arm, grabbed the hair with a meaty hand, and wiggled it like the corpse was a puppet. Once he had grip of a good hank of hair, he grabbed the jaw with his other hand and opened and closed the mouth. "I was pissweak, I was. Don't be like me, bitch. You'll fucken die," he said in a mockery of a female voice.

"Kee id ayay," Katy said, shaking her head, scared to enunciate properly for fear she'd mash the maggots crawling within her destroyed mouth.

He came closer with the naked corpse, dancing with it, spinning it around like he was the ballroom dancing king of this scungy room. Flies circled around them, and the things crawling in his skin rippled.

When he was within touching distance, he positioned the corpse's pale dead face only millimeters from Katy's. Flies travelled between her and it. Maggots fell from its nostrils and its mouth and plopped onto her with terrifying regularity. She tried to buck away, but there was nowhere for her to go. With each plopping thwack, her fear and anger grew. So far, she'd had to suffer the indignities with no chance of reprieve, and although her hands and feet were bound tight beneath the bench she was strapped to, she promised herself she would do everything she could to escape. If she couldn't get away, she would die.

The man continued speaking for the dead girl, using a high-schooler's impersonation of a nagging woman. "You should be mighty proud, love. Do you know how many times he's had soft sheilas in your position suffocate? Sheilas like me can't handle all the little darlings filling their mouth and their tiny airways."

He tossed the body into the corner and covered it.

"Not you, though, love," he said. "You're stronger than her. She didn't last a day. Probably didn't want to. Probably didn't appreciate the boon she was given. You're gonna wanna make sure you do." He leveled his face on her, deadpan. "Yeah, nah, you're gonna have to make sure you do."

He was right. She was stronger. Her grandpa had known she was strong. When she'd told her father of her plans to travel the path in Grandpa's book in the days after Pop's funeral, he'd only allowed it when she'd allayed his fears with promises she was a big girl, promises she was tough. It was time to prove it.

She grunted once, nodding.

"Something to say, do ya?" He leaned over her and the creatures burrowing in his jowls, in his temple, slithered and passed beneath the pores they had created like eyes sliding past peepholes.

She had to make him think she was going along with his story. "The medeors," she said, chewing maggots with the movement of her jaw.

"You wanna know about 'em?" A glint appeared in his eye. He crossed his chest like a catholic. "They're special, they are. So special. Don't believe the bullshit the authorities spin about this area being volcanic. Don't get me wrong, it fucken is, but there *were* meteors. Those pricks just don't want you to know anything if it could bring their power into question. 'Course, the holes the meteors left have filled with groundwater. But the special shit is what's in 'em. It's *Him.* From the heavens, all the way to here, and he needs an Earth-born messenger."

"You?"

He grinned. Shook his head. Scratched his balls. "Not me. I thought so once, but in the grand scheme of things, I'm fucken nothing. Just a right-hand man."

Fearing the reference might be lost on him, she tried to say Renfield: "Ren-feel."

"I dunno what the fuck you're trying to say. Doesn't matter, though. You'll get nothing from me, love. No point trying your bullshit on me. I couldn't give you a baby if I wanted to. I tried it before, and I was punished for my transgressions."

Panic exploded in her chest. Her shoulders heaved and her ribcage swelled as she began to hyperventilate.

He laughed. "Not with you. Don't you worry your pristine little pride. The damage was done long before then." He walked to the shelves and as he reached for a flashlight, he leered at her. A lunatic grin had stretched across his pallid face. His eyes had assumed a zealot's glint. "Do you wanna see how he punished me?"

She didn't. She wanted him to leave. Wanted him to let her try to puzzle out her escape.

He stepped closer, and his hand dropped down to his crotch, his fly.

She shook her head.

"Don't be embarrassed, sweetheart. It's not like that. I want you to see how He loves me and how He guides me." He dropped the zip, clicking it past the teeth slowly, grinning as he did so.

He was relishing this new insult, but what he pulled out from between its golden fangs left her gagging. It was purple and bruised and oozing. Pocked pores like the ones scarring his face dotted its grisly length and it writhed with movement as things wriggled inside it.

She puked. Able to turn her head only slightly to the side, the thin trail of vomit dribbled down her cheek. She spat maggots as she hocked everything she could, and he laughed.

He returned it to his pants, and he laughed and laughed and laughed.

When he was done, he knelt beside her. Flies circled them both and his acrid smell penetrated her nostrils, searing them with his sweaty stench. "I know it's a sign," he said. "I only need to deliver you. It said the new coming will be born through me. At first, I thought it was literal, but . . . " he cast his eyes to the ground. "But it's not. Yeah, nah, I'm only the courier." He snatched her face and twisted it until she looked him in the eye. "Do you understand?" he asked. "You're a gift, and your mate with the stupid haircut is only here to provide the seed for your fertile little womb. Once he has . . . " He pressed two fingers to her head and mimed a gunshot. "He's fucked."

She jerked as he leered at her, and for a moment, she was certain the frame she was tied to tilted, one leg coming slightly off the ground. She veered her weight back to where it was, hoping the prison would steady. If she could tip it over, maybe she could get her hands free. If he suspected anything, her only chance would disappear. She desperately tried not to look at the door, not to let him think she was entertaining notions of running.

Frantic, she cast her eyes to his. "Ow ong."

"Not long, love. Not long at all." He stood and retrieved the flashlight from the shelf. He inspected the wounds in her gums, nodded, satisfied, and flicked the light-switch as he left the room, bathing her in a darkness full of carrion-eating flies and maggots.

Without being able to touch it, Kip could see how infected the knife-wound and the disgusting sore around the broken bone jutting through his skin had become. Unlike Katy, his head wasn't tied in place, so when the door between his prison and Katy's burst open, he lurched towards his captor.

The big man had a definite strut in his step, and he beamed as he cottoned onto Kip's attention. He raised his fingers and waggled them in a perverse wave. "How's the arm going, Cobs? Them maggots working their magic?"

Kip let his chin drop to his chest. No matter what happened here, he was totally at this fucking lunatic's mercy. If the cops were coming, they'd be too late. Even if this crazy bastard dropped dead from a heart attack, the infection in his arm probably meant it was lights out within the next couple of days.

A huge peal of thunder drowned out whatever it was the big man said next, and the rain, somehow, picked up again. It drummed on the tin roof with renewed fury, and it trickled in again through the holes in the ceiling. The ever-present whine of the flies seemed to disappear beneath the torrent. "Fucken pissing down, mate!"

He wished this prick would stop calling him 'mate'. It was a mockery, a corruption of the word.

"When we're done here, things are gonna be pretty bloody different for you." The spectacled man moved to the workbench nearby, grabbing a jar of flies. "In a way, you're gonna be kinda like this jar. Just a big empty vessel for God."

Within the jar, massive black shapes buzzed chaotically. The man held it by the lid and beneath the insects, white maggots squirmed across a ball of rotten meat. He popped the lid off and the flies careened out, joining their brethren as they flitted around the room.

The man watched them with wonder in his eyes. "Fucken magic," he said. "When I dropped 'em in here, they were little pupae, unable to do fuck all, but now look at them. Reborn to travel around and consume all the horrible, rotten, and dead things."

He stepped as close as he possibly could to Kip, so close their noses were touching.

"They get a bad rap, flies. It's not fair. All they do is eat what's turned to corruption and take it away. Without 'em, the world would be a much dirtier place."

Kip tried to tell the man to remove the gag, but it effectively muffled his words.

"You're a talkative little cunt, you are, aren't you?" The man pulled the gag down. "What are you gonna do? Beg me to let you go? Tell me you won't tell anyone? I've heard it all before, and the reality is the only place you're going is along shit creek in a barbed-wire canoe."

"People are expecting me. You've gotta let me go."

"Fuck, mate, you're pissweak. You've told me several times, and if it's not clear, I don't give a flying fuck. They'll learn to live without you." He flicked the gag into place. Kip winced at the man's hot breath.

Kip tried to headbutt him, desperate to lash out, to hurt him, to let him know it couldn't be this easy, but as soon as he launched his head forward and his weight pulled on his broken elbow, he screamed, becoming dizzy.

The big guy laughed.

"Here, I was saying about vessels and shit; about cleaning the world of corruption. You're gonna play a part there. You get to be Joseph, the father of an immaculate conception, and your son'll dispose of some of the shit around this place. First, though, I wanna show you something."

He reached into the jar and pulled out the rancid meat. He held it to his own face and after placing the jar down gently, he spread one of the pores in his cheek with two practiced fingers. He waved the meat above the orifice, a tantalizing treat, and then, with deliberate movements, a maggot, pearlescent and fat, poked its head into the air. It hovered wistfully before the meat as if considering its options. It struck. Like a snake, it latched onto the meat and tugged at it, tearing a chunk free.

Despite its miniscule size, Kip saw it all in fine detail. The thing had fucking jaws. It had teeth. Whatever species of fly the dude was mucking around with, they weren't normal. They were extra predatory, extra alien. He didn't think the weight in his guts could drop any lower, but while he was already scared for his life, a new kind of fear bled into him. Listening to metal for most of his life, he wasn't naïve when it came to other-worldly horrors, extra-terrestrial monsters, and demonic bullshit. Whatever this crazy bastard had found, it was bad news and Kip needed to be more proactive. If he was going to wait for the cops to rescue him, he may as well give up. He had to engineer a chance to escape.

"Pretty fucken grouse, hey?"

Kip shook his head. "What are they?" he said around his gag.

"They're special," the guy said. "A species you only find around here. Around the meteors."

Kip thought the crazy bastard had forgotten all about the meteors. But after seeing the jawed creature come out of the prick's face and latch onto the meat, he began to suspect why the guy was so infatuated with them.

"Anyway, I came to get a look at how your elbow's healing. You've got a big hike coming up, and I need to know if it's gotta come off or not." He grabbed the elbow with his meaty palm and squeezed.

Kip bellowed as white-hot pain speared his elbow. Searing tendrils of agony stabbed into the swollen flesh and pus oozed from the wound. Tears bloomed in his eyes, and he beat the back of his head against his rebar prison. Flies exploded into flight around him. The rain beat down as the man continued to squeeze.

After what felt like an age, he let go. "Yeah, it's pretty fucked," he said. "If it's not any better when I'm done running some errands, we'll chop the cunt off. Gonna have to."

Kip watched the bastard leave. His lip quivered; trembled. His shoulders heaved, and then he let the tears of rage and frustration swallow him whole. He was going to die here.

SEVEN

THROUGH THE RAPIDLY beating wipers and streams of water running down his windscreen, Pastroni could see the bunting tape the cops had strung around the area. Instead of slowing to inspect it more closely, he drove straight past the abduction site, checking his rear-view mirrors as he put distance between himself and it. When he approached the next dirt road heading off the highway and back towards his property, he pulled off the road and stopped to think.

Already, the waters were higher than they had any right to be. He'd taken a chance coming out here, but he was getting worried about the boy's claims his friends would have called someone. He'd gotten cocky, and he had to see this as a fuck-up. Still, he couldn't change it. He had to assume if the cops had found the bike, they would come looking for him sooner rather than later. Logic dictated they'd go to the BP and his vehicle would be on camera. So would the bike. The scratches and dents on the Ranger's paint wouldn't hold up to scrutiny, let alone a forensic inspection. If he was going to make this work, he had to stop fucking around.

He reached under his seat and retrieved a handgun. He checked it was loaded and veered onto the road. With the rain continuing to fall and the creeks spilling over, the roads would close within the next few hours. Provided he didn't have to kill any cops before he got home, he could start the journey to the morass and get this show on the road. The fact the waters would cut them off would buy him time, and by then, it would all be over anyway. He'd be wading into the swamp and giving himself to the creature before they ever found him or the missing kids.

The sound of the roaring engine slowly diminishing as it ventured into the distance was music to Katy's ears. As soon as it was gone and only the constant static of the rain, the howling wind, and the roar of thunder was all she could hear, she braced herself and threw her weight to the left.

The frame she was tied to rocked, but only slightly. The flies made disgruntled attempts at flying away before landing where they were before. The maggots in her desecrated mouth continued wriggling, unfazed by the commotion.

She rocked to the right, ignoring the strain on her cramped and aching muscles and the dull complaints of her many bruises. She threw her weight to the left. This time, the frame shifted, and as she thought it was about to topple, it caught; held fast. Fuck, there must be a bolt or a screw anchoring it to the ground after all.

There was a scraping metal sound and the frame dropped into a central position.

Immediately, she threw her weight in the opposite direction, and this time, the metal screeched before a buckling sound reported and the entire frame crashed to the ground.

She thudded down awkwardly on her side, crunching her arm beneath the metal. She screamed in pain, and one of the hooks in her mouth was ripped out, taking what felt like a chunk of flesh with it. Katy caught her breath. Whatever she had been strapped to had made a terrifying crash. She was certain the man would return any moment.

She lay awkwardly on the wet concrete until she felt ready to figure out the next phase of her plan. Water dripped through the ceiling, and she could see it starting to seep under the corrugated-iron sheeting of the giant shed they were trapped in. It was impossible to know how long she'd been imprisoned, but it was long enough for the rain to seriously encourage a flood.

Muffled shouts came from the room behind her. Kip was alive; had heard her clatter to the ground.

She moved her legs. If, as she hoped, the frame was built around a tripod structure like most weight benches, she should be able to loop her tied ankles over the central leg near her feet. She pushed her legs out and heard something metallic chink against the frame. As she expected, it seemed to only catch in one place. She kicked her tied feet out again. They caught again. Fuck it. Fuck it, fuck it, fuck it.

She was strong, goddammit; she wasn't going to die here on the floor, tied in place like a wild animal. She kicked again. Again. Again.

And then the sound of an engine appeared on the horizon.

She moaned wordlessly and tried not to break into fresh tears. Once the panic disappeared, she realized it didn't sound anywhere near as gutsy as the engine of the big man's car. His roared, chewing petrol. This one purred, conserving it. She held her breath, hoping against hope someone had tracked them; someone had seen the bike, or the woman at the servo had reported yesterday's strange events and the cops were coming to chat to the perpetrator; tell him to stop hassling the tourists.

And then the engine sounded close. It was on the property outside, it had to be. Tires squelched on soft, wet grass. The engine died. A car door opened.

Voices.

She bellowed. Screamed. Howled.

Kip did the same in the room behind her.

Someone called out. "Hello?" They sounded confused, unsure whether they'd heard what they thought they had.

"In 'ere! In 'ere!" Damn what he'd done to her mouth. She feared she would never speak properly again. It all hurt so much, and every time she tried to use her jaw, the maggots wriggled, and the pain grew. "El!" she called, "El-me!"

Someone banged on the door.

"Hello, are you in there?"

In the back room, Kip bellowed louder than before. Still wordless; still gagged, he gave it everything. Katy responded with loud moans of her own. Her first; they had to come to her first.

The banging on the patio door became insistent and she called out, long and wordless, desperate for them to open the door. In the room with her, the flies buzzed and swirled, angry.

And then the glass of the sliding door shattered with a huge crash. The ancient safety glass clattered to the floor, skittered across the concrete, and a man in an industrial yellow raincoat stepped through. His face dropped in shock when he laid eyes on her, and she screamed. She was free. She was free. She was free.

"Holy fucking shit," he said, gesturing to someone. "Get the fuck in here and help me." Another man appeared behind him, following him through the ruined door. In the room next door, Kip continued screaming and the first man reached a hand for Katy to hold onto. He told the other man to take care of her. He then opened the interior door while the first man lifted the bench free, untangling her chains.

Through tears of joy and shock, she watched him scrabble around on the bench before returning with bolt-cutters. "It's gonna be okay," he said. "I'll get an ambulance here. You're safe."

There was no way they could wait. "Ave do go," she said. "E'll ee ack." She scrambled to her feet and made her way to the broken door just as another engine came roaring along the road. Seconds later, the engine grunted, as if suddenly working harder. The maggot-man had seen the SES vehicle her rescuers had come in.

The man who'd untied her came running behind her. "Get in the car," he said. He had a mobile phone in his hands. He chanced a look at the shed. "Bruce! Hurry up. Someone's here."

She hobbled across to the vehicle, but instead of joining her, the man who'd freed her stepped towards the gate, holding a hand to the man, expecting him to slow down as he approached.

It didn't happen.

The blue Ford bounced through the gate, accelerating as it entered the property. It ploughed straight through the SES worker, who rebounded off the grill, folding unnaturally as he hit the grass and skidded away. The vehicle didn't stop. It followed the skittled hero's trajectory and drove straight over him. The front left tire chewed the man's leg, ripping flesh and bone away and mincing them, before driving over his ribcage, splintering bone and squashing his face into the soaked driveway.

The first volunteer, Bruce, appeared as he exited the shattered glass door. He had Kip with him, and flies billowed out behind them.

Caught between the Ford and potential rescue, Katy needed to be as far away from the maggot-man as possible. She skirted around to the front of the SES vehicle, a bright orange Toyota Landcruiser.

The maggot-man stepped casually out of his vehicle and raised a handgun. It reported twice as he casually blasted one of the Landcruiser's tires. The air escaped with a hiss and Bruce and Kip ducked inside the shed.

Her kidnapper looked at her, looked at the shattered glass door, and raised his eyes to the heavens. He pointed the gun in her direction. "Don't fucking move, bitch." He stepped closer, and as he approached her, Bruce, the SES volunteer, came sprinting out of the shed, making a beeline for the vehicle.

The man spun and fired at him.

The bullets went wide of the mark and Bruce ducked down out of Katy's line of sight. She had no idea what he was doing, but she wasn't hanging around to find out. If her kidnapper came out on top in this fight, there was no question where she'd end up.

She sprinted towards the forest in the distance, full of adrenaline, ignoring her aching bruises. Gunshots and shouts exploded behind her, and she could only hope the man wasn't shooting at her.

Dimly, she was aware of Kip calling for her, but she couldn't stop. She needed to escape the droning flies and she needed to escape the man who reveled in their presence. Since the last volley of gunfire, no shots had rung out. She didn't know whether it meant he was dead or not, but she didn't dare look until she reached the cover of a huge eucalyptus's thick trunk.

When she looked again, she saw Bruce jump out of the driver's side door, firing a flare gun at the man. It speared wide of the mark, but in the distraction it caused, he raised the fireman's axe all emergency vehicles like his carried. He needn't have bothered. The muzzle of the maggot-man's gun flashed and a single shot reported. Bruce's brains exploded out of the back of his head.

His body collapsed.

Katy ran.

Pastroni grinned. The bitch could run all she wanted. It didn't matter. There was nowhere for her to go. The murky swamps would have swelled and bled right across the forest already. If she thought she was going to traverse those unmolested, she had another thing coming.

The other one, the bad haircut who'd turned out to be a massive fucking pussy was standing in front of the shed like a stunned mullet, clutching his arm and, apparently, appraising his options. If he had any brains at all, he'd have ignored his boo-boo and run for all he was worth. Sure, Pastroni would have shot him, but the way things were going, he was going to experience pain to make a bullet seem like bliss. What could you do, though? There was no accounting for cowardice.

"Probably best you don't go after her, mate. Probably best you go and lie down and forget about her. She's not going very fucking far."

As the rain pelted down, running through his clothes and soaking him to the bone, he could feel the maggots crawling under his skin becoming agitated.

It didn't matter, but the boy was clearly caught in two minds. The fact he hadn't run meant he was too hurt to try it. If he made a break for it, Pastroni could easily toy with him, and it wasn't like he needed him in pristine condition. So long as the little cunt was breathing when they got out to the morass, shit would be fine.

"Go on, mate, get in your bed like the low dog you are."

Kip stepped further away from the broken patio window. He looked furtively at the man; at the open gate in the distance urging him to make a run for it. The bastard hadn't bothered trying to stop him. He hadn't needed to. Kip had blown his chance when he'd watched Katy run and hadn't followed her. When she'd disappeared into the foliage at the rear of the property, he should have taken his chances. But if he did, he'd need to run straight past the man. Considering the fucker had already killed two people in the last few minutes, Kip didn't like his chances, especially when his arm flared with pain every time he took a step. If he tried to run, the agony would be unbearable. The alternative, though? More mutilation? More maggots?

Already flies were swarming on the splashes of brains and blood sprayed out across the soggy grass. Rain pattered down on the mess, washing the smallest patches away, but Kip couldn't help but stare at the flies as they wriggled and flitted from bloody spot to bloody spot. By rights, they shouldn't be out here. Everyone knew they couldn't fly in the wet; water stopped their wings from working, so why were these ones able to traverse it? What made them have jaws? What made them so fucking special?

His kidnapper watched him staring at the flies, then moved closer to the SES worker he'd shot in the head, opening a passage. "Faster than a bullet, are you?" the man asked. He chuckled and nudged the corpse with his boot. He grunted, looked at Kip and grinned.

Kip stepped towards him, hoping he could feint him out, step one way and duck the other. If he could lead him on a little chase, he might be able to get in the vehicle. Might be able to make a break for it and run.

The murderer walked towards the other corpse. From his vantage point, Kip could see this one was much more mangled.

Kip stepped towards the Landcruiser.

The man spun, fired a bullet into the front left tire. "Don't be fucken silly, mate."

Kip ran. As he suspected, needles exploded in his elbow. Every shunting footstep brought more pain, but he couldn't stop. Wouldn't stop. He stepped left like he was on the footy field in his schooldays. He stepped right.

The gun sounded and wet mud splashed beside him.

The gate wasn't far ahead. He kept zigzagging, swerving. He was probably seconds away from a bullet in the spine.

The gun sounded again. Splinters exploded from the gatepost.

His elbow roared. He could feel every jostling bump, and finally, he was aware of splashing footsteps behind him. He increased his pace and reached the road. Left. Right. Water was spreading across the road in both directions.

The gun sounded again and this time he felt the bullet whizz past his ear. He turned left; began splashing across the tarmac and then the big guy was on him. The bastard crashed into his legs from behind, and he went down. He was desperate to protect his arm from the impact, but he couldn't make it happen. He landed on it and the agony was worse than anything he'd ever felt.

His captor spun him over with rough hands. The maggots in his face were wriggling and poking their heads out of his pores. The stench of death emanating from him was as sweet and rancid as the contents of any sun-ripened trash he'd smelled on bin-day. And then he realized the bloke's fist was coming. It crashed into him, rocking his head, and the next thing he knew, he was being dragged back inside the property.

EIGHT

INSIDE THE TINY police station, Nguyen waited patiently for the printout to come through. When it did, she spun out of her chair, and shook the car keys. "Coghlan, we've got an address for a blue Ford Ranger, and it's not far from where we found the bike. Let's go."

"You're bloody kidding. Bureau of Meteorology's put a flood warning on the river. It's climbed two meters already."

"Yeah, so hurry. Leave your coffee. Those kids might be alive."

Coghlan rolled his eyes and took one last swig. "Fuck you and all the heroic fiction you must have read as a kid." He walked towards the car-park. "We'll go as far as we can, but you're not risking my arse crossing any bridges if they've gone under."

Knowing full well he was right, she wanted to slap him. If only one of those kids was still kicking, they needed to move quickly. "Imagine if it was someone you loved," she said. "Would you want to risk it then?"

He paused. "You know I didn't mean it like that, but you can't take all this shit personally. This guy, he's got nothing to do with—"

"With what?"

"C'mon, let's go."

"No, say it, *Chase*. Fucking say it."

He shook his head. "We don't need to fight. We need to get going if we're going to make it before it's too late."

She stared daggers at him, confident he was going to mention her brother. "Start the engine," she said, throwing him the keys. "I'm gonna get something to help us."

In the storage room, there were two inflatable kayaks. She lugged the first one out and threw it in the trunk of the Pajero.

Coghlan stuck his head out of the driver's side window, ignoring the pelting rain. "You can't be fucking serious."

"You know I am." She went inside the building and grabbed the second. "You will be too if you need to be. I know this looks fucked up, but I'm not gonna walk away from here knowing I could have done more. We're here to help people. To stop the bad guys. You can bitch and moan all you want because I know you'll come through when it matters, but if you think we're not going out there prepared for anything, you've got another thing coming."

He pulled his head inside the vehicle and cranked it into gear. As soon as Nguyen was inside with him, he hit the sirens and swerved onto the road.

Nguyen punched the address into the GPS and fired up the stereo. The opening chords of Nick Cave and the Bad Seeds' "Papa Won't Leave You, Henry" rumbled out of the speakers, and she cranked the volume. As Coghlan accelerated, she stared into the driving rain. They could only hope they weren't too late.

Kip's whimpers became screams of outrage as Pastroni shoved him to the concrete. He landed heavily on his broken elbow. The water leaking in from under the old corrugated-iron walls coated the floor in a thin sheen. Kip had thought the pain couldn't get any worse, but excruciating agony once again proved him wrong, sending shockwaves through his system.

The man's laughter boomed around him, echoing off the walls.

Kip looked up, eyes swimming with tears of frustration and agony. He wiped them clear with his good arm and saw the meat statue his kidnapper had made. The decaying ruinations of death couldn't hide the victim's age. Wet in places, mummified and dry in others, her body writhed with corruption and feasting maggots. Flies alighted on her wrinkled breasts, crawled in and out of her nostrils, mated on her exposed flesh.

He scrambled away from the disgusting thing. Is this what the man had planned for him? He shuffled farther away from the grotesquery, trying to clamber to his feet, only to feel a sturdy boot press down on the small of his back.

He fell, looked at the man and his lecherous grin. "Say g'day to Mummy Dearest then, bloke."

Kip didn't comprehend.

"My mum, you stupid bastard, say g'day." He waved at the

corpse. "Hello, Mummy Dearest. We're gonna make it work this time. This is the daddy, right here. I know he's not much to look at it, and he's kind of a bitch, but it doesn't matter. He won't need to raise the kid with all his modern ideas. We've got *real* values covered on this end."

"You're fucking crazy!"

"We've been through this. Lots of people have said it, but we'll see who's crazy once we get out to those craters. We'll see . . . "

The man grabbed Kip by the collar, dragged him to his knees and threw him against the wall. He pulled zip-ties from his pocket. "If I need these, I'm going to cut your fucken tits off, d'ya hear me?"

Kip tried to pull away from his grasping hand, but the man struck him fiercely across the face. "Now, let's show you how we're gonna find your girlfriend."

"She's not—"

A kick to the ribs blasted the air from his lungs. His weight dropped, and again the pain in his arm rushed through his body. This time, he vomited. Considering the fact he'd not eaten since the last time, he was surprised at how much puke there was.

The man pressed a finger to his own lips; laughed. He tapped Kip's chops with powerful fingers and pointed at the remains of his mother. "Now, mate, what you're looking at there is far too good for the likes of you. Old Mumsy gets to live on. You'll have a legacy, but you won't be here to see it. Make sure you watch, though, because I'm gonna show you some real shit."

Kip watched the bastard turn to the flyblown corpse and tried not to panic. The butterflies in his stomach, the ache in his head, and the constant dull agony coursing through his body—not to mention the roaring fire in his elbow—made it hard to think, but he was certain he should have run. Certain he was doomed.

The man knelt before the corpse. Kip couldn't fathom how crazy the bastard was. Sure, the flies were something else, in particular the maggots with their toothed maws, but this level of insanity could only come around through the most fucked-up course of events.

His kidnapper made the sign of the cross, reminding Kip of life at school. He didn't have time to finish the thought. The room became alive with flies. They flitted and buzzed across to the corpse and the kneeling man. They swirled and gathered behind the dead woman.

It was incredible. They gathered as if they were a hive-mind, forming arms which moved as the man mumbled his prayers, and Kip was sure he'd lost his wits. If he didn't know better, he'd swear the fly-man was humming and dozens of maggots had emerged from his rippling and pallid flesh. While it was difficult to see from this angle, what was perfectly clear was the maggots crawling within the corpse had emerged. They stuck out like arms of coral and extended themselves towards the praying man. They opened their mouths and began to hum. The man reached his palms out, a happy clapper at the world's most fucked-up church service.

The flies hovering around the corpse began to land on the killer. They covered him from head to toe, and he disappeared beneath a rippling, convulsing skin of shiny black flies.

The man stood, walked to the door, and pointed in the direction Katy had sprinted. The flies peeled off him, taking to the air in an angry black cloud. The ones that hadn't clambered over him poured out of the room and joined the swarm of flies following the kidnapper's command.

As the last fly buzzed out the door, Kip could see the maggots protruding from the prick's flesh; was certain they had watched the flies with interest. Disbelieving, he turned to the corpse. There, they also protruded, and then, as one, they turned to him, showing their tiny, fanged mouths. They hummed.

The man strutted across the room and kissed the corpse on the forehead. He spun and looked at Kip, grinning, not maliciously, but clearly proud of his work. "And to think, you haven't been proved wrong about those meteor fields yet. I bet we're shattering a lot of the bullshit you believe today."

He pulled a knife from his belt and raised it to Kip. It was the same long, heavy weapon he'd had earlier. Kip cringed at the sight of it, sure the bastard would use it again.

"Don't," he said. "I'll do what you want." He hated himself. He was a fucking coward, but he couldn't figure out any other way to escape. He was too wounded. Too defeated.

"You don't have a choice, fuckhead. This is insurance, though. It's time to go."

When Katy came to a breathless stop and took in the forest around her, she couldn't help but wonder what she'd been thinking. The ground beneath her feet was covered by wet, ankle-deep slush. It sucked at her shoes with every step and the wind howled through the trees, surfing through the foliage and breaking on her soaked frame, chilling her to the bone.

The maggot-man hadn't bothered to follow her. The thought was unnerving. When she'd heard the last volley of gunshots, she'd had to look back, only to see him firing at the running Kip. She'd chosen to delve further along the outskirts of the forest, but she didn't seem to be getting anywhere. She thought there must have been more properties out here, but there were none on the horizon. There were cows and there were fields, but she'd begun to realize this was one of those plots on massive acreage you saw in Outback movies. No one was coming to rescue her.

The water was getting higher and higher. It cascaded down any raised surface, and it couldn't be long before the floodwaters surely rose to meet her. She'd have to take her chances and keep pushing along until she came to road. If she couldn't find a property, road would have to do. From there, she could push towards town, escape this crazy bastard and call the cops to help Kip, if he was alive. Until then, she would need to do what she could to escape.

She wasn't sure exactly what the crazy fuck had meant by saying she would have a baby. At first, she'd thought the obvious; the cheap horror of so many rapey B-grade films and thrillers, but she'd seen his ruined cock. He'd never be using it to hurt or wound others, or even to pleasure himself. It was a broken thing, and he was for all intents and purposes a eunuch.

He could and would hurt her, though. He already had. She'd seen him kill. She'd seen evidence he'd killed before, and she needed to escape to make sure there was justice for those he'd murdered. She wiped a stream of rainwater from her hair, from her eyes, and tried to see into the hazy distance.

Beneath the gusting wind, beneath the relentless beating of the rain, and beneath the infrequent lowing of the cattle in the fields, she was sure she could hear a swarm of flies. She had to be imagining it. Flies couldn't navigate through rain. The raindrops ruined their delicate wings, so there was no way the black smear in the distance could be real, could be closing the distance between themselves and her.

There was no way she wanted to test the theory. She turned into the forest, and once again ran as fast as she could on the sloppy detritus of the flooded forest floor.

NINE

KATY DUCKED UNDER a hanging branch and turned. The buzzing was loud. The odd fly broke from the swarm, homing in on her like a missile. As far as flies went, some were large, easily spanning upwards of three or four centimeters. They were easily as big as the giant one from the shed. They careened into her, thwacking her like small stones, plunging their proboscises into her like needles. She slapped them away, but she couldn't keep this up.

Their terrible zizzing was close. It echoed off the surrounding trees and buzzed in her head. It was angry and full of menace. If she didn't know better, she'd swear there was a voice in it, one urging her to give up and give in. She couldn't. The ground was slippery, and the terrain was dangerous, but she couldn't stop. She didn't know the forest, she didn't know where she was going, but she had to keep running. Her lungs felt like they were going to collapse. Her legs hurt, her head was a mess. Her reservoirs of hope and determination were rapidly dissipating, but she would sooner die running and fighting than she would on her knees.

Ahead of her, she noticed what must have been a natural game-trail used by kangaroos and other types of wildlife. It ran alongside a small creek flowing with gushing water. She pushed for it, and as she tried to put on another spurt, she felt the muddy ground slide away. She lost traction and she slipped painfully to the treacherous surface.

In seconds, the flies swarmed her. Their buzz filled her ears, drowning out the sound of the rain on the canopy and she felt them biting her and crawling across her flesh, looking for soft, weak places. She'd had enough of the disgusting little bastards. Maggots crawled in the damaged flesh of her mouth. Given the chance, they would lay more eggs in her. She screamed, swiping at them and squishing them in the palms of her hands. They were so big, they felt like mice or rats, not like the disease-carrying vermin they were.

She rolled onto her back and looked up, seeing a man-like shape made from oscillating black flies standing over her. She crushed more of the foul creatures in her palms, swiped away the ones biting her, tried to push herself to her feet. More of the bastard animals peeled off the humanoid figure to take the place of the fallen.

It came forward, closer, and the voice she thought she'd heard earlier spoke clearly. *Give up,* it said. *Give in. Give yourself to us. Give life to us again.*

This couldn't be happening. She reached into her mouth and yanked out a fat maggot. She pinched, grinding it between thumb and forefinger and howled in wordless frustration. She shouldn't have. As soon as she yawed her mouth, flies zoomed inside. She covered her face with her hands and chewed, mashing them on swollen, infected gums, desperate to kill them. Their ichor ran over her tongue, down her throat. Their legs crunched like sticks and disgusting ooze overwhelmed her tastebuds.

Give in.

More flies burst inside her mouth.

The voice became laughter. The shape stepped closer. She lunged for it.

She clenched her fists, crushing flies, but more were coming from the forest around her, piling into the shape, making it more dense, more terrifying. To think she'd come out here to prove the people of the Outback were not killers and weirdos. To think she'd wanted to write a book about kindness and compassion. Instead, she was here, fighting this thing; witnessing this, this fucked-up shit.

The flies melted out of the shape and swerved around her, forming a large sphere. She spun as it zoomed towards her, shielding her face. Flies washed over her, plunging proboscises, stabbing, biting, consuming. The creek, fast-moving and dark brown with rainwater, beckoned.

She had to hope there were no crocodiles here. Had to hope they hadn't found their way into this part of the Outback. Bull sharks she'd take her chances with. She dove in, hoping the water would keep her safe.

As they approached the dip, Coghlan slowed the vehicle right down. For the last thirty minutes, they'd been driving across road at least an inch-deep with rainwater and run-off. He peered through the windscreen, making a show of the effort he was putting in to get across.

Nguyen shook her head. Tutted. She pressed a hand against the interior of the windscreen, ignoring the rapidly beating wipers, and pointed to the white post showing the depth of the floodwater. It was only a meter. They'd be fine to cross it in the big Pajero.

Her partner grunted.

"What?" She'd had about enough of him slowing them down. "If you don't want to drive it, you can let me do it. We'll get across easily."

"What if the road's washed away?"

"It's a dip, not a fucking bridge. Drive."

He accelerated, and the vehicle pushed into the brackish water. The water immediately flowed over the grill, but the car kept pushing forward, and in moments, they were past the obstacle.

"Happy?" Coghlan asked.

"I don't get it. Do you want to catch this fucker or not?"

He sighed. "I do, but I'm worried you're being rash. We got an address so why not wait? You think he's gonna close shop because he gets flooded in? We could be at risk out here. If we get ourselves in shit on bad roads, what good are we to anyone?"

She wanted to fire up, but she'd long ago learned getting pissed off at colleagues did nothing. Life was better if you could at least listen to them. "I hear you. I do. I hear you."

"But?"

"But my worry is less about him shutting shop than it is him realizing he can't have loose ends around if the SES or good Samaritans pay him a visit."

The car thunked over a fresh pothole and rocked from side to side.

"Okay, so talk it through. What's that shit look like? We don't know these kids are alive."

And there it was. The glass-half-empty view. "More importantly, we don't know they're not. We've got no bodies. No bodies at all, so I'm working on the proviso there are kids out here in trouble, and the whole reason we started this career was to do something about this kinda shit."

"You think he's got a farm full of kidnapped fruit pickers out here, do you?"

The rage in her grew. She was practically blowing steam. "Fuck. You." She picked at her collarbone. "We spend our whole careers giving out speeding tickets and fining broke-arse locals for missing headlights, and the one time we actually have a chance to make a difference, to possibly save lives, you wanna play it safe. Fuck that."

"I got a wife and kids at home who'll be worried sick about me out here. Who might need me to lay sandbags or squeegee rising water away from the house. This isn't—"

"Like I said, those kids might be alive, and if he thinks they put him at risk he'll fucking kill them. You know this as well as I do, so if you want to be the kind of cop who makes everyone hate us, who justifies them calling us pigs, pull the fuck over. I'll take the kayak and go on alone. If you can do that, and you can still sleep at night, go right ahead."

Coghlan accelerated. A short distance up the road, another dam had broken its banks. The brown water swirled over the road. Coghlan didn't try to slow down. He hit it fast, and the water fanned out in a huge spray.

"There you go," she said. "Easy."

"Okay," Coghlan answered, "but I'll tell you one thing. The Kanga Creek Bridge is under and if we can't cross it, we're done."

She glared at him. "Drive faster."

He pressed the pedal and the engine roared.

"Don't worry about her, fuckhead. She'll be back with us in no time. Deadset, I'd be mighty surprised if the flies haven't found her already. She's hardly gonna be Steve Irwin once she gets out in the forest, is she?"

Kip was finding it impossible to phase out the taunts. All he could do was continue putting one foot in front of the other and hope to ignore them. His arm was so, so sore. If he somehow got out of here alive, he was under no illusions about keeping it. Not only were there things wriggling in the flesh, but horrible venous trails of black were creeping down from the elbow to his fingers, climbing his upper arm, spreading tendrils of infection into his shoulder. Pus oozed from the wound. He would be amazed if the whole thing didn't fall off without help at this point.

Ahead of them, a small bridge stretched over what would usually be a thin irrigation ditch. Colonial in style, it was another decaying victim of the lack of care and attention rotting everything left on the property. The man with maggots in his face pulled Kip towards it by a rope he'd looped around his neck, splashing across the ankle-deep water and forcing Kip to pass straight over it. On the other side, a goat track punctured the wall of foliage hugging the fence-line.

"Keep fucking going. We've got a fair hike ahead of us yet."

One of the maggots in the bastard's jowls had been hanging half-in half-out of a pore for the better part of a minute or two. It swiveled to look at Kip. It was fucking huge. If Kip didn't know better, he'd think it was some kind of grub or caterpillar. He returned its gaze, wishing it would climb out of the man's face and fall to the ground so he could squash it underfoot.

The hideous creature bared its teeth at him and then withdrew inside the bastard's face; it rippled the flesh, moving like a mole beneath the skin.

Kip shuddered. The things growing inside his own decaying flesh would no doubt grow to the same size. Walking forward, he let his gaze drift to the ravaged limb. In several places, his skin bulged, but with his good hand fastened to the rope tied around his waist, he couldn't press them, pinch them, or try to dig them out.

Bile climbed his throat, and he choked down vomit. He wanted nothing more than to escape, to burrow in the skin like a junkie and root the vile creatures out of his flesh; to eliminate them and the idea they were corrupting him, growing in him, evolving into the massive flies aching to do the man's bidding.

They passed into a deeper stretch of forest, and the hammering din of the rain deepened as it became a sound emanating from the canopy above him and not one from the splashing ground at his feet. Even if his friends had called the cops, it was too late. If someone had found the bike, it was too late. He'd practically condemned himself to death with his failure to act.

The rope tightened, momentarily choking him, and he realized the man was yanking on it. "Stop daydreaming and hurry the fuck up." The man pointed to a foothill ahead. "We're going up there, and I can't drag you all the fucking way. Put some lead in your pencil and man the fuck up."

Kip hated the term. It was the kind of bullshit thing the jocks and his old man—the absent prick—would say. No one he knew was as tough as his mum was while his prick of a father had been whacking her senseless seven days a week. "Manning up" was a joke, but the fact it reminded him he could still feel anger meant he could channel it.

In the past, he'd channeled his outrage into music, into fast riffs. Here, he'd have to channel it into action. Katy—now there was a tough bitch—had leveled up as soon as she saw her opportunity. Regardless of what was happening, she was giving herself a chance, however slim. Kip couldn't say the same for himself. He had to. He was probably going to die, and if he wanted to survive, he needed to be more like the women in his life. They'd proven they were survivors time and time again.

Looking at the foothill and the soggy, muddy goat track leading to it, he might have a fair chance to put things into action in the immediate future. It would hurt like fuck, but if he thought of the arm as something he needed excised from him, he might be able to make it work.

"Come on, cunt. Get a fucking move on. You've got a date with destiny."

"Righto, fuckhead, tell me where you want me to go. Let's get this shit done with." Kip wasn't sure he believed the words and his temperature rose as he glowed red with anger, momentarily blotching away the sickly taint crawling over him, but it was a start. He'd finally showed at least the tiniest bit of guts. He could do it again.

The big man holding the rope laughed. "Look who grew a dick. Bloody hell, I'm almost impressed."

Kip strode past him, climbing the first steep steps. The muddy ground beneath him squelched and his footing slipped as he pressed his weight down.

The man reached out, steadying him. "Easy, tiger. Don't want you falling, do we?"

Kip grunted, hoping the man had no idea what was about to happen, and regained his stride.

TEN

KATY ROSE FROM the rapidly gushing creek, gargling water, trying to dislodge the creatures crawling in the torn flesh of her mouth. The flies were on her in an instant.

Travelling in a tightly clustered ball above her as she ducked and dived through the creek, it swooped as one hive-mind, clattering her and driving her underwater.

Already short of breath, she couldn't stay under much longer and she needed some other way to combat the buzzing shape. Unfortunately, helpful ideas weren't coming.

She surfaced again, splashing as much water as she could at the swarm, hoping desperately to break its focus on her and drown some of the insects in the process. Despite catching a few with her frantic splashes, most of the flies dodged the waves and redoubled their efforts.

She dove beneath the surface and kicked her legs. Gliding underwater, unable to see clearly in the murk, she crashed headfirst into a boulder. She rose, white agony ringing in her skull, and tried to shake her head clear. Warm blood immediately daubed her lips, gushing from a gash on her forehead. Its copper scent filled the air.

The flies hit her again. Their proboscises piercing and prodding as they landed.

Give up. Give in. Give yourself to us and birth Him.

She waved her arms. Swatted flies off her face; her torso. Tried to ignore the taunting voice and turned towards the deeper water. She crushed a fly in her hand, feeling its sticky insides in her palm and immediately clutched another. She stepped past the spot where the boulder was submerged. Something like a fish or an eel touched her ankle, its cold flesh surprising her.

She squealed, flinching away. The mass of flies barged into her again. The water moved oddly. Something touched her ankle again, more firmly this time, then, a dull black shape crested, breaking the brackish surface. Water sluiced down the contours of its scaled hide.

She lunged for shallower water. The people out here could keep their secrets. They could keep their flies and their hospitality and their fucking monsters. There was some creature from folklore, some aquatic beast inhabiting the billabongs and gullies of secret places, but she didn't want to know the truth of it. Whatever bullshit the maggot-man had been alluding to, she didn't want to write about it in her book. Didn't want to find out any more about this land so far away from the one she thought she knew.

She tugged her leg away, pushed through the biting flies, and made for the bank.

She could hear the water splashing and cascading, but she wouldn't turn. Wouldn't give it and its thousands of voices the satisfaction. Wouldn't face it.

The flies hit her again.

Give in, the cacophonous voice in her mind said. *Turn. See.*

She couldn't. She wouldn't. She ran.

A thin, groping tentacle slapped the ground beside her. It was long and barbed, and she couldn't bear to look. She swatted flies and wiped the blood gushing down her face. She ducked and weaved through the trees, hoping the flies would leave off and allow her to run.

They swooped hard at her legs. The impenetrable buzzing cloud should have been no more resistant than mist, but it was real, and it was solid, and it slowed her gait; forced her to stumble. As she righted herself, they crashed into her back and knocked her to the floor. If she had time to think, she'd be amazed flies could be so powerful, but all she could do was splash across the wet ground and try not to slip in the mud.

She rolled, scrambled for deadfall to pull herself to her feet with and ran again. She had no idea where she was. All sense of direction had been lost after fleeing whatever it was in the water.

She paused for breath, swatting the flies, conscious their constant bites had left blisters and her forehead was bleeding. Lethargy swelled in her aching muscles, and she wasn't sure how much farther she could run. Somehow, she needed to get to the edge of the forest, head for the road, but for as long as the zizzing, buzzing voice of the flies was needling her, she didn't see how she could.

Give in.

This time, it came like a whisper and when she turned, the swarm had once again taken a humanoid shape. The flies, large and small, swirled in tiny circles, somehow keeping position in a great chain of carrion-eating cohesion. It reached an arm out, but right when she expected it to step towards her, it began to levitate.

Aghast, she stepped backward as the shape rose. Its droning became hypnotic, looping in a pulsing beat. Mesmerized, she listened as she watched, and then a foot that wasn't a foot swung out and connected with her chin. She fell again, putting her hand on a fallen branch. She pulled it, and saw it had leaves. Broad leaves. She swung it through the shape and cut a huge swathe through the hive-mind. The harmonized buzzing broke into angry spasms of noise. Again, she ran, knowing all too well it would follow her.

Kip breathed heavily as he approached the top of the foothill. If he could make the right move, he'd have a good chance to make a run for it. The foothill tapered off into a flat plain, but he had no intention of moving forward. He doubled over and waited for his captor's taunts.

The bastard didn't disappoint. "Big show-off rushes to the top and now he's fucked. What a shame." He treaded up, using the rope around Kip's neck as leverage, almost throwing him off balance.

"Here," Kip said, pulling the rope with his good hand. "If you're going to kill me, you may as well tell me your name." With any luck, a false sense of security for the motherfucker would do wonders.

The maggot in the murderer's face reappeared as he eyed Kip, presumably mulling the question over. "I'm not gonna kill you," he said. "Won't be my job."

Kip watched as the man reached the lip of the foothill. Kip jumped, meaning to slide down the way he'd come. In seconds, he was slipping faster than he had any right to. Stabbing blasts of pain shot through his arm. His head swam. Resistance tugged on the rope, and then it gave.

The murderer swore loudly.

Kip reached the bottom and saw the big fella crashing after him. He didn't know exactly how the prick had fallen, but it looked like he'd tried to catch the rope and been pulled forward. He was sliding face-first. The slick mud facilitated his pace, and Kip scrambled to the side.

When the bastard crashed painfully to the bottom of the foothill, his shoulder crashed into a tree. He let go of the rope, and Kip, unable to yank it with any effectiveness, half scrambled half staggered away. He made it to his feet, pulling the slackened loop of rope over his head—not an easy task with his broken elbow—and moved as quickly as he could.

He was slow and the man would come after him, but just as the old adage suggested, *it was better to die quick, fighting on your feet.* The path they'd taken to get here was mostly under a shallow stretch of water, but he could make out footprints in the mud. He followed them, ignoring the man's shouts.

"Get the fuck back here, cunt!" the bastard shouted. "You'll fucken suffer for this!"

Kip kept moving. Every half-jogged footstep fired an explosion of pain in his elbow. He was rife with infection, but he needed long enough to plan. Long enough to put distance between himself and Ivan Milat's more fucked-up cousin.

Something boomed behind him, and something whistled past his ear. A patch of bark on a nearby eucalypt splintered. The hammering rain quickly doused the ghosting curl of smoke.

"Next one goes in your back, you fucken dog!"

Kip pulled in behind the tree and tried to hold his breath as he waited for the man to approach. He didn't know exactly what he could do, but he'd have to do something.

"Gip!"

The shout was quiet. Coming from somewhere in the distance, it was half-smothered by the sound of the rain, but Kip had no doubt who it was: Katy.

The man's footsteps came closer.

He waited until he was sure the bastard was as close as he could be, then Kip spun out of his hiding spot, and charged with his head lowered. The joke when he was a kid going to punk shows said you could call a good headbutt a Liverpool kiss. If true, the blow he struck counted as foreplay. He hit the bastard fair in the nose; felt it crush beneath his forehead and heard the filthy prick scream.

He ignored the pain in his own head and sprinted towards the sound of Katy's voice.

The rapidly approaching buzz of what sounded like an entire army of flies followed.

Nguyen smiled as Coghlan navigated the last stretch of the Kanga Creek Bridge. The swirling water behind them had tugged and pulled at the vehicle, but thankfully its snorkel and raised chassis had got them across. The brown water eddied and swirled, and she couldn't help but think of the commercials no doubt playing on television right now. IF IT'S FLOODED FORGET IT, they'd be saying. "Told you she'd be right!" She punched the dashboard happily. "Now, fucking floor it."

Coghlan grinned. "I hope for your sake we get this fucker because we're caught on this side of the creek now."

"What do you think the kayaks are for? I knew you weren't gonna let me cross without you, and you wouldn't leave me on my own. You're an arse, but you're not a harmful one."

He only gaped at her.

"Come on. Let's go. If he thinks he has to flee, he'll kill survivors first. We've been trying to find these people for months, and now we've got the biggest break we've ever had. If any of them are alive . . . "

Coghlan accelerated, and they continued driving until they reached the address. Despite the flood having submerged the grass verge, the fence posts on either side announced its location. The positioning of the SES vehicle beyond the gate—not to mention its wide-open door—suggested everything was not okay. Coghlan smashed the accelerator and they burst onto the property, water jetting out to either side of the Pajero.

As soon as he parked beside the broken sliding door of the Titan shed, Nguyen dragged a large duffel bag into the front seat and threw a vest on. While doing so, she heard Coghlan swear. He'd walked around the front of the abandoned Landcruiser, and when she joined him, she saw why. There was a dead man on the ground. Flies carpeted his face, their shiny black abdomens bulging like pearlescent scales.

"Come on," she said, gesturing to the shattered patio door

leading into the shed, and as she stepped towards it, she saw the second body. This one had clearly been hit by the car. The legs were crumpled like bent straws, but she couldn't imagine how the body would look. It too had disappeared beneath an undulating layer of flies.

Coghlan raised his own weapon, and together they slipped inside the shed.

The smells of blood and decay hung heavy in the air, redolent and thick. The drone of flies buzzed within the structure, and occasionally, one would zigzag by them as it flew around on its errands.

"It doesn't smell good," Coghlan said.

She wanted to snap at him. The stench in the air could only come as the result of something dead.

She made her way through the room and opened a door. There, as it swung open, the hideous figure of a propped-up corpse leered. She spun away from it, gasping. "Get the fuck in here, Chase. Now."

"No," he said. "Look." He pointed his gun at a mound in the corner of the room. A single pink Converse sneaker poked out from the bottom. The foot beside it was bare.

Bile rose in her stomach as Chase lifted the sheets. Maggots and beetles crawled across Dana's naked body. The dried orifices of multiple knife-wounds were plain to see. She couldn't tell Colin and Debbie how Dana had been left. She'd have to invent her lie later, though. Coghlan needed to see the corpse in the next room. "We'll get her later. Look in there."

He crept past. "Holy fucking shit. It's like he's made a statue of it." A long maggot peered out of the dead woman's nostril, then plopped to the ground. Coghlan stomped it with a heavy boot. He held a hand up, clearly listening. Nothing but the ever-present zizz of flies and the drumming of the downpour sounded.

Nguyen inspected the body. Somehow it was mummified, but the charnel smell of death seeped into every one of the room's surfaces. The floor was sticky with dried blood and bodily fluids, but she couldn't pull her focus away from the desiccated face of the dead woman. Gray hair curled from the scalp like furry mold on rotten fruit. The jerky-like appearance of the skin made telling the age difficult, but this was no young woman.

"Who you think this was?" she asked. "We got any old ducks on the missing register?"

Coghlan grunted, peering through a crack in the tin wall and inspecting the contents of the room next door. "Fucks me. Probably thousands of them."

"Don't be a prick. You know what I mean. Local ones?"

He returned and inspected the corpse. "No idea. Could well be someone who knew him. Might be no one knows she's dead."

The jaw dropped open and a dozen maggots crawled out, plopped to the ground, and began to wriggle towards them. They took turns stomping them, and then the corpse began to scream.

Nguyen spun, amazed. From the pores of the corpse, a hundred maggots stretched towards her. Their tiny mouths opened—something she didn't know could happen; wasn't entirely sure was possible—and screamed. She hopped back, reflexes driving her reactions and pointed her gun at the corpse.

"When the fuck did maggots start making noise?"

Coghlan pulled her away from the figure. "They don't," he said. "Least not when they're rolling around in my wheelie bin."

The wire holding the corpse's hands in prayer groaned.

Nguyen stepped away from the dead woman, making the sign of the cross on her chest, shoulders, and forehead. She shuddered and watched the dead woman; not sure it hadn't moved.

When it remained motionless, she made her way into the next room, covering Coghlan as he took point.

In there, they saw the shelves lined with jars of flies. Some of them were humongous. Way bigger than any she'd seen before. A variety of bloodied tools sat in haphazard fashion on the bench. "This is him."

Coghlan didn't bother responding. He went to the door on the far side of the room. After peering out of the window, he beamed. "If I'm seeing what I think I'm seeing, there might be at least one living captive with him."

Nguyen swore. Where were the others. She inspected the pair of footprints Coghlan had found and looked out across the property. She pulled her hood tight and stepped outside. From this angle, the cars were around the corner, and as she approached, she saw another trail of swampy footprints beneath the layer of water coating the ground. They led into the forest.

There was a plink and a crashing sound in the room where the dead woman stood. Nguyen looked at her partner, and together they glanced towards the room, waited for the sound of shuffling. "What the fuck is going on here?"

Coghlan shrugged, raised his gun, and stepped towards the room. "Body's fallen." He looked around as if expecting to see someone in there.

"Is someone else here?"

Coghlan shook his head. "Nope. Think the wire's old. It's pretty rusty."

Nguyen took a deep breath. "Let's go," she said. "I make at least two of them alive. We can worry about this creepy bullshit later."

Coghlan tightened his own hood and fell into step beside her.

ELEVEN

PASTRONI SLAPPED THE wet ground and roared. How the fuck had *that* little cunt given him the slip? How the fuck had the girl gotten so far? For God's sake, he couldn't cock this up again. Last time had been the worst. The flies had hurt him then; punished him, leaving him mutilated and sick. With these floods making sure God could get anywhere He damned well pleased, things had to be sorted now.

He cocked his ears, listening for the buzz of flies in the near distance. When he was satisfied he'd located them, he walked towards them. "Oh, little lovebirds, I need to show you something."

The screaming insects sounded angry, and then, he heard shouting. The girl.

Just as he thought, the little bitch had been too thick to get away from here. Had fallen into the trap of running into the forest and not away from it. She'd elected to avoid the open road and had instead doomed herself into a death-march towards the ever-widening morass.

If the thing in the craters hadn't already begun moving, its coming wouldn't be long.

He dropped to his knees, made the sign of the cross, closed his eyes and raised his hands like a happy clapper. Seconds later, he began to hum, quietly at first and then with more effort.

A fly landed on his jowl. Another alighted on his face, and as it picked its way across his scarred cheek, a maggot protruded its head from the sanctuary of Pastroni's plentiful flesh. The fly brushed it, and from behind his closed eyes, the bastard saw what the greater swarm could see: the boy, blindly making his way across waterlogged ground as he tried to locate the shouting girl. They weren't far from the squat little government building near the edge of the swamp.

He laughed and walked in that direction, scratching the base of his neck where the horseflies had fed, and called out once again. "Oh, little giiirrrlllll, don't you wanna see what sights I have to show you?"

Dozens of maggots, meaty and gray, protruded from his face now, but his eyes were closed, and he could only feel them dancing their snake-charmer dance. What he saw was communicated to him through the maggots by the flies as they closed in on his captives.

He stood, listening to the urging buzz of his beloved pets and, stroking the barrel of his gun like a cock, walked in the direction the maggots poking out of his face pointed. The time was almost here.

Katy heard Kip splashing and blundering through the foliage as she shouted for him. The poor bastard looked deathly ill. She couldn't believe he was managing to traipse through the forest. While she'd hardly come away from her meetings with the maggot-man unscathed, she only needed to look at Kip to know he'd had it worse. Right from the moment he'd been thrown off the bike to the moment when the maggot-man had smashed a motorbike helmet into his face, and to whatever indignities he'd had inflicted on him in the shed, Kip had suffered brutal punishment. She had to get him out of here.

She was already pressing a finger to her lips and pointing in the direction of the fly-buzz when he saw her and called her name. She angrily shushed him. "Fies! Gogga go."

He collapsed to his knees. Looked at her sadly. "Your mouth . . . what did he—"

She cut him off. "Don urry. Gogga go." She dragged him to his feet, careful not to touch his arm and led him into a thicket. The heat emanating from his body was furnace-like in intensity. If she touched his arm, the pain would be unbearable, and from a glance at the swelling and the veiny black shapes crawling towards his neck like sprawling tendrils, he would probably lose the entire limb.

"It's flooded," he said. "We can't escape."

She'd considered the small concrete building she'd seen, but it was locked and was far too easy a landmark for the maggot-man to rely on. She had to get them to the house. To the shed. She could get them out of here, and there was no fucking way she was going any deeper into the forest. Whatever the thing with the tentacles had been, she didn't fancy meeting it a second time. No way.

A human shout came from the distance, presumably the maggot-man. Only last night she'd been talking about the fact the people in the Outback here were harmless. If he hadn't come along, hadn't seen them when they stopped to get out of the rain, she'd still be on her spiel, and he'd still be out here taking lives and doing whatever the fuck he was doing with them.

He'd said he was impregnating her, but she couldn't believe him. She'd seen his ruined manhood, and he was barely more than a eunuch. She could scarcely believe he could piss out of it, let alone get a hard-on. And what the fuck was with this pseudo-religious bullshit?

Although, to him, it wasn't bullshit, was it? She'd seen something in the water; had narrowly avoided its tentacles and had to believe the maggot-man had seen it too. Further panic crept into her bones. That thing was what he was calling God, and he planned to give her to it. Regardless of whether it could do what he thought it could, it was quite clearly predatory in nature, and Katy doubted her chances of surviving the ordeal.

"Maggud-man."

The swelling drone of the flies may as well have signaled a hunting horn. "Fies. Und ush! Esh go."

She half-dragged him out of the thicket, further towards the direction she thought the maggot-man's property lay. She splashed forward through calf-deep water. The whole forest was pretty much under, and the water was gluggy and black beneath the dark, stormy sky and the canopy's sodden gloom.

Kip, for his part, did what he could, pushing forward, half jogging, half stumbling as she dragged him. He was running on empty now, but all they had to do was get away from the man. Katy had no doubt the maggot-man knew this place well, but if they kept moving, they could do it.

Ahead, the ground dipped in a natural channel and the rainwater gushed through it, connecting with the creek. She wanted to turn back; knowing the monster might be there, but the droning flies and the shouting maggot-man meant she wouldn't. Not in a million years.

She approached the channel, keeping Kip steady, petrified of what might be waiting.

Something moved in the water. Something turned, letting the black fluid trickle down a scaly hide. Her heart thumped, gaining speed as her throat and mouth went dry. A long tentacle windmilled, a centipede spinning, trying to sense prey with its antennae.

She ducked left. Kip followed behind, and then, a shadow fell upon them. The drone sounded overjoyed as the flies began to cycle around and form a large black orb. Any second now it would reshape itself, manifest the shimmering humanoid figure, and if it caught her again . . .

You're going to have a baby.

No! She wasn't. She was going to get the fuck out of here or die trying.

"Gip, un."

She ran along the edge of the channel, staying far enough away to be clear of any probing tentacles, but she didn't want to lose sight of the creek. They had to cross it to get to the property, and with the floodwaters rising, they had to do it soon.

The flies swooped. They crashed into her, sending her sprawling in the gunk and the muck and she screamed in pain. She scrambled up, pulling Kip with her, fearing she was going to have to let him go and run for her own life if he couldn't save himself, but, again, he got up. He might have been next to useless in her attempt to escape, but he could take a beating.

She swatted at the flies, beating them away, trying not to let them into her mouth, her nose, her ears. They whirled around her, cyclonic, whipping her, biting her, searching for an opening.

When they couldn't find one, they closed on Kip, and she pulled on his good arm, desperate to help him escape their suffocating embrace.

Inside her jaws, wriggling things vibrated in time with the buzzing insects.

In her peripheral vision, the scaly hide rippled through the water. No tentacles were visible, but it could only be a matter of time.

"The cat's dragged in a proper pair of messes, hasn't it?"

His voice was distant, and it took her a moment to spot him beyond the swirling black cloud of the flies. He stood between two dead trees, his palms held in supplication. His eyes were glassy gray orbs the color of maggots.

"I don't know what He sees in you," he said, gesturing to the slithering shape in the water, "but He's told me it's gotta be you."

He raised his gun. Fired.

Katy felt the wind of the bullet as it blew past her leg. She didn't give him a second chance. She ran, leaving Kip to his fate.

Nguyen heard the shot crack and echo through the forest. She pulled her own gun and ran in the direction it came from, splashing through calf-deep water.

Looking back, she motioned for Coghlan to follow. Running was tricky with a bullet-proof vest on, but she persevered. In her mind's eye, she could see her brother somewhere out here, not as the pile of bones he would surely be, but as his sweet self, cherubic, as he was in the photos her mother had left on the walls of the family home.

A second shot cracked. Time passed and a pained howl followed.

Kip only realized the shot had missed when Katy piss bolted. He watched her go, shocked she hadn't hit the deck. Seconds later, through a cavorting cloud of black insects, the paperbark of a nearby tree exploded in a wet cloud of debris. Katy kept running, and the filthy fucking prick—the maggot-man, if he was to use Katy's name for him—gave chase.

Everything seemed to slow into a meandering blur. If the maggot-man wanted to catch her, he would have to cross Kip's path. The young guitarist had been useless so far. All those kids who'd ragged on him at school, mocked him for being small and puny and a weak little pussy who only liked punk music because it let him vent his anger at the world, at his father, at everything, would be proven right if he did nothing. Without it ever feeling like a conscious decision, he waited until the bastard was within reach and dove for him.

Somehow, trying to protect his injured arm, he managed to

latch onto the bastard's belt with his good hand. In the slippery mud, the man fell easily and together, they crashed to the floor.

Kip howled. His elbow had jarred against the dude's knee and the pain rocked him. He didn't let go. He held on. Even if he was doomed, he could buy Katy enough time to get away.

With the maggot-man writhing beneath him, the flies doubled down on Kip, beating into him, seeking the fleshy parts of his body and biting, but Kip held on. Every second counted. Every moment could be—

The man swung the gun, pistol-whipping him right in the sternum and the wind blew out of Kip in a whoosh. He blinked, his vision blurring, and he felt the man scramble free; felt him pull away like a slippery fish.

"You fucken prick!" The man was snarling, growling, panting, but Kip managed to swing his good hand and tap the guy's ankle. Again, the maggot-man fell in the mud, dropping the gun. This time, it was Kip who wriggled. He clambered over him, reaching for the weapon, knowing it was his best chance of survival.

The fucker punched Kip's elbow.

Kip screamed.

The rain beat down. The flies circled. The man who could talk to them wrapped two meaty hands around the wrist of Kip's wounded arm and yanked.

When Kip roared in agony, the bastard pulled again, dragging Kip through the mud.

Kip could feel the flesh stretching, could feel the jagged bones tearing into the meat and the tendons and ligaments giving way beneath the pressure.

He tried to dig his feet into the ground; tried to clutch at the man's ankle, but it was no good. He couldn't compete with the pain.

The maggot-man dragged him to a thin tree, not much more than a sapling. He laughed, and then there was a thud.

The pain Kip had thought incapable of getting worse rocked him like an explosion.

Dimly, he was aware the bastard was bending his arm at an unnatural angle, using the tree as a fulcrum, but more importantly, there was nothing he could do to stop it.

TWELVE

KIP'S SCREAMS PIERCED the air. They climbed above the pounding rhythm of the hammering rain and the rumbling thunder. Katy had to rescue him. Sure, escape would allow her to live, but what kind of life would it be if she had to picture Kip's final moments in nightmares for the rest of her life?

She looked across the rising swamp spanning the forest floor and thought of the rippling shape she'd glimpsed only moments earlier. It could be anywhere in the murky brown water and the idea of it appearing when she was knee-deep in sludge filled her with fear. And then, when another of Kip's screams pierced the air, she looked behind her. Knowing what she had to do, she dropped her head and returned to the place she had come from.

Kip's screams became louder as she approached. The reason was clear. The maggot-man had a foot on Kip's ribcage and was yanking his bad arm with the intensity of a weightlifter tossing battle ropes. Blood leaked through Kip's shirt and the monster bellowed as he heaved, his intentions clear. She hovered behind a tree, not wanting to announce her presence, and realized she was too late. All she could do from this distance was scream for him to stop. When she tried, only a squeak crept out of her mouth and before she could redouble her efforts, the arm came free. Tendons and veins stretched and snapped like gristle and fat, and a spray of blood splashed through the air. The droplets were quickly beaten down by the rain and washed away in the churning tide.

Behind the tree, she was sure Kip was done for. Dead. To her surprise, though, the kid who simply refused to die moaned and rolled on the wet ground.

The maggot-man licked his lips and raised the arm above his head like a baseball bat. Katy couldn't watch as he brought it down, but she heard the thwack as it landed on Kip. He belted the guitarist with it again and again, and Katy slumped to the ground, watching from between her fingers.

She scanned the floor for anything she could hit him with, and there, seemingly forgotten, the man's gun lay not far from where he was beating Kip to death with his own truncated limb.

Tears blurred her eyes. Maggots rollicked in her gums. Somewhere in the floodwaters, a giant creature slithered and swam. She had to grab the weapon. Had to use it.

She forced herself forward, slowly at first, before her own momentum took her closer. Trying to creep, trying not to sniffle, trying not to let him know she was coming, she ignored the thick runnel of snot dripping from her lip and edged forward, knowing she should move quicker. Something beneath her right foot moved and coiled. She slipped. Crashed to the ground.

The maggot-man turned. "There you are! I knew you wouldn't go far without lover boy." He cast his eyes across the ground in front of her. His mouth dropped.

It didn't matter. She was moving again.

"No you fucking don't," he said, but yes, yes she fucking did. On hands and feet, crawling like a beast, she scrambled for the gun and as he dove, sprawling his hand toward the weapon, she grabbed it and pushed herself to the side.

Rolling with it, she pointed it like a light-gun at the arcade. The man was getting to his feet. She was backpedaling, but she pulled the trigger.

The gun cracked.

A red hole appeared in the bastard's chest.

He looked down. Pressed a hand against it. "Ah, shit. You bitch," he said falling. As he splashed onto the wet ground, his arms flipped out sideways. He lay, motionless but for the flies loitering on his greasy flesh.

She climbed to her feet. Pulled the trigger again. This time nothing happened. She dropped the gun and pulled a heavy stone up. The ground sucked, refusing to relinquish it, but she was determined. She lifted it high, fell to her knees beside the dying man, and crashed it into his face again and again and again, stopping only when the rock was too slick with blood and floodwater to hold onto.

She clambered across to Kip. His chest heaved in ragged breaths. She pulled her shirt off and tried to wrap the gored stump of his arm in a tourniquet.

"My arm, my fucking arm," he said, weeping openly. "My guitar. My band."

Fresh sobs heaved her shoulders. He was dying.

And then she heard the thick buzzing of the flies. They poured from the trees around them and coalesced into a roiling orb. From within it, a voice, abrasive in her mind, spoke. *Give in*, it said.

The shimmering, swirling orb of black insects was already reshaping itself, forming something once again vaguely humanoid in shape. Katy wasn't surprised when it moved as if it was walking towards her. No, the surprise came when it pointed at something behind her.

Kip's glazed-over eyes went wide. "Run," he said.

Behind her, in all its hideous glory, the black thing from the water had stretched to its full height. It towered above her, its head as high as the canopy. Its segmented and slimy body oozed pus and saliva. Its tentacles and legs writhed like a centipede's. The pearlescent folds of flesh hanging from its carapace stretched and clenched, stretched and clenched.

Nguyen had full sight of the creature as it burst out of the water, rearing upwards like the maggots when they had spewed out of the dead woman's face in Pastroni's shed. One moment, she was looking past the man's bloodied corpse, her interest in the girl her prime concern, and the next she was coming to a running stop, holding a hand out to stop Coghlan from running past her.

Muck and slush foamed off the gigantic monster as it stretched its head into the canopy. Its body undulated as it pushed its length out from beneath the surface with long legs tipped with wicked spines. A sucking sound accompanied the ever-present buzzing. The earthy aroma of standing water followed. Tentacles rasped and writhed out from beneath the revolting flaps of skin hanging below its fanged head.

A black shape Nguyen had hardly noticed before levitated, and she realized it was a swarm of flies hovering in the shape of a man. The girl reeled, desperately trying to backpedal while pulling her bleeding friend with her.

The creature's circling tentacles seemed to be getting closer to the girl, and Nguyen didn't need a PhD in zoology to know it was preparing to attack.

She raised her gun.

Coghlan put a hand on her shoulder.

"Together," he whispered. "On your count."

It was the fastest three-count she'd ever offered. The two of them burst out of the foliage firing their weapons at the giant thing. Gobs of flesh exploded from it, and it raised its tentacles before slapping them onto the ground in a spray of mud and muck.

"Keep firing! I'll get the kids!" she yelled, edging closer.

Coghlan did so. He might be a dick in real life, but when it mattered, he'd never let her down.

Nguyen edged in, keeping her weapon on the creature, firing periodically as she grabbed the girl's arm. "I'll help! Drag him back! Into the trees," she bellowed at the panicked girl.

The girl's eyes went wide, and she tugged harder at the bleeding boy.

Nguyen helped her get him to his feet and as she turned with him, hoping to get him to safety, a tentacle speared into the boy's stomach, plunging in like a hypodermic needle. A second wrapped around his neck, holding him upright, and she saw the tentacle begin to pulse, peristaltic, chugging, sucking something from his innards. Another harpoon tentacle flew towards him. This one smashed into his groin and immediately began ripping and tearing before it too started to suck, vacuuming gore and bodily fluids into the beast's belly.

Blood washed down his legs; spilled over the sucking tentacle. His screams of agony were almost unbearable and then, there was peace below a loud angry buzz of flies. Nguyen would never forget the next thing she saw, and she'd never forgive herself for being grateful it stopped his wailing. The flies piled into his open mouth. There were millions of them, and they must have filled his lungs, his stomach, his trachea because they kept flying in, never stopping until they came out of his ears and nose.

She fired her gun at the monster, aware Coghlan was calling to her, telling her to run, and then a third tentacle came hurtling towards them with the speed of a bullet. She could do nothing as it slammed into the kid's face. Blood and bone sprayed, coating her, and the girl screamed. A thick black spike protruded from the back of the boy's skull. His body went limp and the tentacle in his guts withdrew; the one in his groin followed, and his guts spilled out through the hole it left behind. His testicles were gone. His manhood was a ruin. The tentacle around his neck uncoiled and he fell, the remains of his skull falling away like a cracked egg. Flies spewed out of the ragged hole where his head had been, billowing into the sky like smoke.

Nguyen tried to pull the girl away and shove her towards Coghlan, but the monster was too fast. The uncoiled tentacle came again. This time, it swooped around the girl's mid-section. She spun, falling to the ground, and then, the tentacle withdrawn from Kip's guts plunged forth again. It penetrated the girl's belly, and as it came forward, Nguyen saw the wicked claws form a barbed and hooked needle.

Coghlan came forward, firing his gun at the monster.

The flies enveloped him.

If she didn't know better, Nguyen would have sworn she heard voices and laughter. She fired at the monster. A free tentacle batted her away. She landed with a pained gasp but struggled straight to her feet. The boy was dead. She couldn't let whatever this thing was do the same to the girl. She had to save someone. She couldn't fail again. Couldn't let it happen on her watch.

She scrambled in towards the monster. Its tentacle was firmly planted inside the girl's stomach, and it pumped in a perverse sexual thrusting motion. Nguyen noticed a second spiked tentacle waving in the air like a scorpion's tail. It jabbed downwards, dripping foaming ooze and she side-stepped as it whooshed past her. The appendage lanced into the ground and as she grabbed the writhing thing, trying to hold it in place so it couldn't come for a second strike, she saw something moving through the tentacle towards the girl's stomach. She'd seen an egg-eating snake in a documentary once, and the movement of the item was similar, only, it was heading away from the monster and into the girl, not vice-versa.

Further up the tentacle, she noticed more of the shapes. Good God, it was planting something in her, and there was no way of knowing how many had already moved through the tentacle.

Nguyen pressed her gun against the fleshy appendage and fired, tearing a ragged hole straight through. White, creamy ooze leaked out of the wound, but the monster kept thrusting, lewdly pumping into the girl. Nguyen fired again and again and then Coghlan was there, pulling the girl away, helping her tear the tentacle in two.

The hooked arm previously trapped in the ground jagged upwards, taking Coghlan through the base of the jaw. His face settled and his eyes stared at her as a sickening crack punctured the air. Coghlan made a gagging noise, and then the spine poked out of his pate like a thorn. As it retracted, half his face came with it in a bleeding strip of flesh. It fell to the ground and Coghlan, who'd never see his family again, collapsed.

Nguyen screamed, firing her gun at the monster and pulling the wounded girl away from the ever-deepening morass. The monster roared and bellowed, but Nguyen continued dragging the girl away from it. They couldn't defeat it. They could only run.

THIRTEEN

AS THE WOMAN pulled her towards the dilapidated house, Katy tugged at the hooked thing protruding from her stomach. She didn't have much clue what was going on, but Kip was dead. The male cop too. The creature had killed them, but it hadn't tried doing the same to her.

She could feel things moving in her stomach. They wriggled and writhed like the maggots in her gums, and she had a suspicion what exactly had happened, and she must be right, otherwise the monster would have trailed them across the wet ground. The thing had impregnated her. It had used Kip and it had bred them. It was some sort of parasite, and she was carrying its offspring, she was sure of it. If she wasn't, it would be coming after them.

"Geddid owder me!" She was screaming, and the cop was shushing her, telling her everything was going to be fine. It wasn't. The thing had infected her and if they didn't get to the doctor's soon, didn't get it removed immediately, its disgusting progeny would grow inside her.

"It's not far," the cop said. "Don't remove it. You'll bleed out."

Katy didn't care. She kept tugging. She could think only of the things moving inside her, trying to find their way to her womb, trying to find a place to suckle and grow. She punched her stomach. Stopped. Threw up.

The cop grabbed her, held her face and stared intently into her eyes. "I know you're scared. So am I but listen." She pointed into the sky, and there, again, below the pounding rain, the fly-buzz was swelling. "I don't know what that fucking monster was, but those flies are coming, and you've seen what they do. We've got to go!"

One of the creatures inside Katy's abdomen moved into a more painful area and she gasped as the cop helped her to her feet and dragged her through the knee-deep water towards the house she had escaped from only hours before.

As she trailed the cop, Katy hoped to see the monster. It was fucked-up, but in a bizarre way, it would make her feel better, would reassure her she hadn't been corrupted by it. Running on adrenaline, she kept an eye open for a black shape floating through the water; hoped every floating log, every tree-stump protruding from the thick brown murk was it.

Whatever the thing was, it seemed to add credence to her kidnapper's stories about the craters being real. Nothing like the creature she'd witnessed, let alone the flies—and their telepathy—could have come from Earth, and if it had come from space, then it had probably come on a meteor; it had to have.

The house appeared on the horizon, and Katy saw the vehicles scattered around the grounds. The ground they sat on was invisible below the brown floodwater covering everything. The house and shed looked like they rose out of a dark brown sea.

"Air's your gar?"

"Other side of the house. I'm gonna call an airlift on the radio. We'll have to hide in the house while we wait for it. The bridge will be under." The cop paused. "I brought a kayak just in case, but . . . "

Katy waved the thought away. There was no way she was getting in a boat.

The droning had followed them as they moved through the forest, and it grew in volume as they stepped out from under the canopy and approached the little bridge leading onto the property. The cops had obviously figured out who he was before coming out here. Maybe they'd found Kip's bike. The cop looked at the cloud of flies hovering towards them and tugged Katy's arm. "Come on." She broke into a run, dragging Katy onto the little bridge spanning the creek, splashing through the water as she made for the Pajero.

Katy was about to step off it when the bridge exploded. A huge fleshy maw burst from the water. The sickly yellow color of a maggot, it thrusted upwards like a crocodile bursting from beneath still water, sending Katy flying.

She landed heavily on the snapped broken tentacle protruding from her stomach and screamed. As the monster roared, the things inside her stomach moved, latched claws into her, and burrowed deeper into her guts, deeper into her uterus.

The cop fired at the creature and chunks of flesh splattered off its hide, but it made no move to attack. It only bellowed and screamed as Katy's belly churned.

She clutched it, hoping to massage the pain away. Her belly had begun to swell. Katy already looked like she was three or four months pregnant.

She screamed. So did the creature. Her belly stretched. Something beneath the surface moved.

The cop grabbed her by the collar and yanked her towards the car. Katy noticed the flies had flown straight past them and were congregating inside the shed.

Nguyen was sure she had lost her fucking mind. Never in a million years had she thought she'd have to deal with the kind of craziness she had seen here today.

The monster remained in the creek. It bellowed and squealed and when it did, the girl's belly bulged and grew. She dragged her towards the Pajero. They might not be able to get out of here, but it was a safe place. The flies were heading inside the shed, so it wasn't an option for shelter, and neither was the house. They'd have to lock the four-wheel-drive's doors and hope the flies couldn't get in.

When she was certain she was a safe distance from the monster, she put her hands on the girl's shoulders. "Listen to me. My name is Lei Nguyen and I'm a detective. We're going to get you medical attention, but I need to call a chopper."

The girl nodded.

"What's your name?"

"Gady."

Katy? "Katy, I know he hurt you and I don't want you to talk because I know something's wrong with your mouth. The man who hurt you, Calvin Pastroni, is dead. We're going to the Pajero. It's the safest place here we can defend. Do you understand?"

Katy nodded. "I gilled im."

Nguyen felt for her keys. She and Coghlan always split the main key and the spare. She had the spare where she expected it to be. Thank fuck for lanyards.

She guided Katy past the crumpled corpse of the SES worker who looked like he'd been hit by a vehicle. From inside the shed, the buzzing was a maelstrom of noise. It was louder than she'd ever heard it, and she didn't want to know what the fuck was going on in there.

The vehicle unlocked with a beep. She got Katy comfortable and radioed through. When she was done, and she had confirmation a chopper would be sent as soon as possible, she pressed a hand on Katy's belly. It pulsed and moved beneath her touch.

She gasped. "You're on your way to the hospital. Whatever this is—"

"Monsher."

She looked into Katy's eyes. They were yellow and bloodshot. Her skin was pallid, and the stench of her was one of miasmic rot. The girl was gravely ill.

"The boy you were with? Was it Kip? We found his motorbike."

Katy nodded.

And then the flies swarmed out of the broken patio door and covered the Pajero in an undulating cloak of beady black bodies. Their horrible zizzing was deafening.

She hit the wipers, but as soon as the flies caught before them were squelched into grime, more took their place.

"Dryy! Ugging dryy!"

She looked at Katy who was panicked, trying to peer through the flies.

"I can't see a thing," Nguyen said.

"Shumun's gumming."

"What? Who?"

"Jush go!"

Katy's frantic breathing came thick and fast, and Nguyen was about to tell her to calm down and say she'd be fine when someone knocked on the window with three steady, beating thumps. One. Two. Three.

A single fly came through the air-vent by the steering wheel.

Nguyen covered the vent with her hand. Another fly drifted out of the windscreen vent.

There was another knock. And another.

Nguyen revved the engine and reversed. She hit the wipers and saw a glimpse of the figure standing there. It couldn't be who it appeared to be. Surely. She was dead. She was a statue. She was human jerky. Yet here she was, walking and stalking.

Nguyen was about to hit the wipers again when the flies began to pour through the vents in a steady stream. In response, Katy screamed, clutching her belly.

There was movement outside the vehicle and as Nguyen felt the flies push into her nostrils, into her ears. She gasped in shock, and they invaded her mouth in a swarm, flying straight into her trachea and down into her stomach.

The dead woman outside punched the windscreen, shattering it. A second punch smashed the glass, and she reached into the vehicle. A deluge of monsoon rain poured through the opening. So did a million flies.

Nguyen struggled to breathe. She coughed. Gagged. Did everything she could to get the flies out of her, including punching her sternum, but it was no use. She opened her door, stepped out of the vehicle, short of breath, fearing she had only seconds to live, and fell to her knees, certain the chopper she heard in the distance would be the last thing she'd ever hear, and she'd never see her brother again. More flies swarmed her.

FOURTEEN

KATY STOPPED SCREAMING when the mummified woman caressed her hair. She couldn't believe how gentle the woman was. How caring. Her desiccated hands didn't matter. Neither did the maggots and beetles crawling through her empty eye sockets. She was nurturing and she spoke to Katy in the same way the flies had, telepathically. Katy didn't know how she knew this, but she did. She was calm and the old woman was telling her things would be fine.

There was a commotion, and then the woman disappeared. Nguyen, wheezing, choking, purple in the face, but somehow alive, pressed her gun against the dead woman's head and pulled the trigger. The weapon reported loudly, forcing the flies to stop their buzzing, but it had no effect.

Flies poured from the hole Nguyen had blown into the dead woman's skull, at first like smoke, and then like a stream of bullets. Katy realized they were using her corpse like a puppet. *Kill her*, she heard a buzzing voice say. *Protect your children.*

Katy screamed. All she'd wanted to do was write a book. A simple book about the myth of the Outback killer, one with interviews and pictures of rustic meals and country pubs, but it wasn't a myth at all. This place was fucking huge, and it was the perfect place for horrible things to remain hidden for fuck knew how long.

She shook her head. The chopper in the sky above them was loud, drowning out the fly-buzz, and she clambered across to the driver's seat. Her belly was huge and swollen and it pulsated with life as she tried to get out of the vehicle.

She reached across to help Nguyen into the passenger seat, but as Nguyen, panting and coughing pulled herself in, the dead woman grabbed her hair with one hand and her chin with the other. The woman, who had to be one of Pastroni's first victims, maybe his mother, ripped her hands backwards and there was a horrible cracking sound. When she was done, Nguyen's head sat at an oblique angle. The top of her spinal column bulged.

Katy could hear voices, but it didn't matter. Something was happening inside her belly. *It's happening*, the fly-voice told her. *He's coming through you.*

There were several loud cracks and the dead woman's head exploded. Flies burst from the wound in a black cloud and buzzed angrily.

"Katy Lewis, we're here to help. Hold still. We've got a stretcher coming."

Her belly was roiling. She fought her way out of the car. The chopper had landed. She could see it. "Ged me the fuggowd," she called.

A paramedic guided her to the gurney. "Are you pregnant?" she asked.

Katy shook her head. "Infession. Paraside."

The wind from the rotor blades was immense, and under normal circumstances, it would have been overwhelming. As it was, though, it kept the flies from coming within range. If the pilot let them rest for a second, the flies would do to everyone here what they'd done to Kip and Nguyen.

The paramedic looked at her quizzically. "Is your mouth okay?"

Katy opened it and pointed at the wounds. Judging by the paramedic's reaction, it looked pretty fucked up.

"Okay, Katy, try not to speak. I'm going to give you a shot. We're going to get you to hospital, but are you sure you're not pregnant, because you've got a horrible protrusion impaling your belly and we want to make sure your baby's okay."

Katy sobbed; squealed. "I dol' you. Infession. Paraside."

The paramedic strapped her to the gurney and said something to the pilot. Another paramedic returned with a police officer, shaking his head.

"Katy, I'm Officer Rex Brown. Do you know if there's anyone else alive here?"

Katy shook her head. "Erryone dead."

The police officer looked away. Spoke to the paramedic briefly.

The paramedics gave her a shot of something, and the helicopter lifted into the sky. With her belly swelling and gurgling, Katy cried.

FIFTEEN

INSIDE THE HOSPITAL, doctors and experts buzzed around Katy's room in a panic. Her belly had swollen to the size of a beanbag. She was weak, and she couldn't understand why they hadn't cut her open and pulled them out yet. To have left them in was cruel, and she was starting to think the doctors wanted to observe; wanted to find out what was happening.

The thing was, whatever the fucking things inside her were, they were wrong. They were demons or aliens or some other fucked-up thing, and they had to come out.

The doctors, wearing full-bodied hazmat suits had separated her from the general public, but no one was talking to her. No one would tell her what was going on. Her mind raced. Her belly hurt. All she wanted was her parents and some fucking answers, but at the moment, it felt like they would never come. Instead, she was stuck here in this sterile room, strapped to a gurney as a monstrous parasite destroyed her.

And then she felt something rupture in her belly. She looked down. This was so fucking wrong. She was a virgin, and while Pastroni had said some shit about the Virgin Mary, the monster could never be a God. She was no more a mother to these things than someone infected with a botfly was. She was a host, nothing more.

Something sharp tore out of her belly, and she saw a long, spindly insect leg reach out. "HEEEELLLLLLPPPP!" she screamed.

She heard movement in the room. Saw the camera in the corner swivel towards her. A hazmat-covered face appeared in the window of the room's only door, and then the pain in her stomach grew in intensity. It rippled, bulged, and tore.

She was dimly aware of several razor-sharp insect legs pushing out of her. She looked like a hedgehog with these spines protruding from her round belly. And then a loathsome maggot-like head appeared from the right-hand side of her abdomen. Its toothy mouth and face writhed with bristles and tentacles as the thing pushed its way out.

It plopped to the gurney, its entire length about the size of a human newborn. Spindly legs stretched and flexed. Its segmented carapace glistened with ooze, and she felt another of the creatures tear another hole closer to her groin.

The first one turned and bit into the flesh it had crawled out of.

And then the pain she thought couldn't get any worse became excruciating. She screamed as several more of the creatures pushed their way out of her, and they all turned to consume their host. The face in the window had been joined by another. The camera in the corner was tracking on her belly.

She screamed for help.

More and more of her belly disappeared as the creatures poured forth from her and then she realized one of the creatures had found its way up the gurney, was investigating the soft flesh of her throat.

Another face appeared in the little window. Surely, they would come in soon. People were good. People were inherently good, and while Katy had been wrong about the Outback, she had to believe scientists and doctors and the government—or whoever the fuck had her on this gurney—would help her.

Katy screamed again for the doctors, for the scientists, for anyone. They were watching. They knew what was happening. They would help. They had to. Surely, they had to. She screamed for them, feeling the creatures tearing at her flesh, and wondered why the men were taking so long.

As she was being consumed by parasites, she watched them watching her from behind the door. She screamed for them to help her again and again and again, and when she realized they weren't coming, she screamed for her parents and for God and when she realized they weren't coming either, she screamed in fear.

If they didn't come, the maggot-man had been telling the truth. If he was right about them, what else could he have been right about? A fresh wave of agony tore up her abdomen as one of the parasites peeled a long strip of flesh from her ribcage to her armpit.

Crimson blood billowed onto the gurney and as another spiny creature ripped its way out of her stomach; she pictured the small building waiting by the edge of the swamp. Its bleeps and blips had been recording something, and as she gave birth to creatures the maggot-man had thought were Gods, she feared not only for herself, but for all humanity.

THE END?

Not if you want to dive into more of Crystal Lake Publishing's Tales from the Darkest Depths!

Check out our amazing website and online store
or download our latest catalog here.
https://geni.us/CLPCatalog

We always have great new projects and content on the website to dive into, as well as a newsletter, behind the scenes options, social media platforms, our own dark fiction shared-world series and our very own webstore. Our webstore even has categories specifically for KU books, non-fiction, anthologies, and of course more novels and novellas.

ABOUT THE AUTHOR

Zachary Ashford is an Australian author, educator, and speaker. His dystopian horror novella *When the Cicadas Stop Singing* was nominated for the Aurealis Award. His other works include the Sole Survivor books, *Autotomy Cocktail,* and *Encampment by the Gorge & Blood Memory*. His short fiction has been published by various presses. His love of Ozploitation creature features has seen him called 'a master of bush horror'. When he's not writing stories about the human condition while surrounded by action figures and monstrous memorabilia, he's listening to death metal, hanging with his amazing wife, chilling with his son, or playing with his cat. His debut novel, *Polyphemus* is due in November from Darklit.

Readers...

Thank you for reading *The Morass*. We hope you enjoyed this novella.

If you have a moment, please review *The Morass* at the store where you bought it.

Help other readers by telling them why you enjoyed this book. No need to write an in-depth discussion. Even a single sentence will be greatly appreciated. Reviews go a long way to helping a book sell, and is great for an author's career. It'll also help us to continue publishing quality books. You can also share a photo of yourself holding this book with the hashtag #IGotMyCLPBook!

Thank you again for taking the time to journey with Crystal Lake Publishing.

Visit our Linktree page for a list of our social media platforms.
https://linktr.ee/CrystalLakePublishing

Our Mission Statement:

Since its founding in August 2012, Crystal Lake Publishing has quickly become one of the world's leading publishers of Dark Fiction and Horror books in print, eBook, and audio formats.

While we strive to present only the highest quality fiction and entertainment, we also endeavour to support authors along their writing journey. We offer our time and experience in non-fiction projects, as well as author mentoring and services, at competitive prices.

With several Bram Stoker Award wins and many other wins and nominations (including the HWA's Specialty Press Award), Crystal Lake Publishing puts integrity, honor, and respect at the forefront of our publishing operations.

We strive for each book and outreach program we spearhead to not only entertain and touch or comment on issues that affect our readers, but also to strengthen and support the Dark Fiction field and its authors.

Not only do we find and publish authors we believe are destined for greatness, but we strive to work with men and woman who endeavour to be decent human beings who care more for others than themselves, while still being hard working, driven, and passionate artists and storytellers.

Crystal Lake Publishing is and will always be a beacon of what passion and dedication, combined with overwhelming teamwork and respect, can accomplish. We endeavour to know each and every one of our readers, while building personal relationships with our authors, reviewers, bloggers, podcasters, bookstores, and libraries.

We will be as trustworthy, forthright, and transparent as any business can be, while also keeping most of the headaches away from our authors, since it's our job to solve the problems so they can stay in a creative mind. Which of course also means paying our authors.

We do not just publish books, we present to you worlds within your world, doors within your mind, from talented authors who sacrifice so much for a moment of your time.

There are some amazing small presses out there, and through collaboration and open forums we will continue to support other presses in the goal of helping authors and showing the world what quality small presses are capable of accomplishing. No one wins when a small press goes down, so we will always be there to support hardworking, legitimate presses and their authors. We don't see Crystal Lake as the best press out there, but we will always strive to be the best, strive to be the most interactive and grateful, and even blessed press around. No matter what happens over time, we will also take our mission very seriously while appreciating where we are and enjoying the journey.

What do we offer our authors that they can't do for themselves through self-publishing?

We are big supporters of self-publishing (especially hybrid publishing), if done with care, patience, and planning. However, not every author has the time or inclination to do market research, advertise, and set up book launch strategies. Although a lot of authors are successful in doing it all, strong small presses will always be there for the authors who just want to do what they do best: write.

What we offer is experience, industry knowledge, contacts and trust built up over years. And due to our strong brand and trusting fanbase, every Crystal Lake Publishing book comes with weight of respect. In time our fans begin to trust our judgment and will try a new author purely based on our support of said author.

With each launch we strive to fine-tune our approach, learn from our mistakes, and increase our reach. We continue to assure our authors that we're here for them and that we'll carry the weight of the launch and dealing with third parties while they focus on their strengths—be it writing, interviews, blogs, signings, etc.

We also offer several mentoring packages to authors that include knowledge and skills they can use in both traditional and self-publishing endeavours.

We look forward to launching many new careers.

This is what we believe in. What we stand for. This will be our legacy.

Welcome to Crystal Lake Publishing—
Tales from the Darkest Depths.